Washington Square Secrets:

Book 2
ALLIANCE

By

Carrie Dalby

*For Debbie Bradley, an ally to many,
and
analog missionary—thanks for the mood
music*

One
1896

Josephine Wolf ran down the porch steps into the night, her black cape fluttering behind her. Nothing was more magical to the five-year-old than the world by moonlight. On All Hallows' Eve, the scents, sounds, and once familiar sights of the yard were transformed into a haunted forest. Tilting her head up, she placed a hand on the witch's hat Miss Sarah had helped her make and gazed at the speckles of white in the inky sky above the towering house. She moved closer to the road and called out under the canopy of oak branches.

"Saints and sinners, I shall be one with you this night and always!"

"You need sinners?" a boy called from the edge of Washington Square Park. "I've got a band of them right here, witchy girl."

A handful of older boys clad in hand-painted devils masks crossed the road carrying baskets in the crook of their arms.

"It's just a baby," the shortest of the devils said, though he was only a head taller than Josephine.

The one in the front was maskless but wore a sneer as vile as the most garish mask. He passed his basket to the nearest villain. "She's old enough to know if she calls for sinners she'll surely get them."

The others laughed and Josephine stepped back, causing the limbs of a gardenia bush to poke at her back through the thin cape as her throat constricted. Had she thought quicker, Josephine could have silently called to her brother with her thoughts, but it was too late now.

"If you scream, little witch, we'll come back later and finish things." The boy—who was beyond grammar school age—snatched her shoulders. Then he twisted one of her arms and marched her north on Charles Street, the others following.

"Little girls are nothing but trouble," one of them grumbled.

"You should know, seeing as you've got three younger sisters."

"One's enough for me," the voice that had proclaimed her a baby said.

"Quiet!" The one holding Josephine tightened his grip as though that would hush his crew.

Her face was wet with tears, but she didn't whimper. The boy led her down an oyster shell driveway off Palmetto Street and jerked to a stop when they were between a deserted house and a wooden fence.

The leader took a step away. "Now pull up your dress, witch."

"She's just a baby, Rupert," the smallest said.

"Yeah, we don't want to see her underdrawers," another complained as she clutched her cape around her trembling form. "She might still be in diapers."

"Y'all are as much babies as you're claiming she is!" The captor pushed the closest boy and they all shifted away from his anger. Nostrils flaring, he turned back to the girl. "Up with it, witch!"

"Save that for a bigger girl," one of the boys said. "We're going to egg her instead."

A blur of white flew toward her. Landing with a sickening *thwack* against Josephine's chest, the gloop slid down her cape, catching the moonlight like snail slime.

The leader laughed and shrugged. "Y'all are pathetic."

As soon as he moved away, there was a volley of eggs. The noises brought the attention of a passing group of younger boys.

"Hey, it's Mat's sister!" A familiar voice in the second group caused her to shiver. Edgar Melvin, the tormentor of the Wolf siblings.

"She's nothing but a naughty witch trying to consort with devils," Rupert, the older ringleader, announced.

"Witch! Witchy Wolf!" Edgar taunted as the seemingly endless supply of eggs continued to rain upon her. "Witchy Wolf!"

Josephine curled into a ball, losing her hat. The shells bit into her knees like fangs. Petrified, she couldn't summon Mathias. But her brother would be nothing against the gang.

"Hey, what's going on?" a voice deeper than any of the boys' asked.

Several kids ran away the same time an egg splattered Josephine's hair.

"Knock that off!" the deep voice said.

"Mind your own business," Rupert retorted.

Another egg hit the side of her head, but she bravely turned toward the boys.

"If you're picking on some runty kid on my street, it *is* my business." The new boy was taller than the others—broader too.

The boys broke rank and removed their hands from the baskets.

"Go find some other kid to rescue, you dirty orphan," Rupert said.

A few snickered, but the majority inched toward the road.

"Grow up, Rupert." The young man tightened his fists. "But for now, get lost. All of you."

"We were here first," Rupert snarled.

Josephine's hero grabbed the shortest devil by his black shirt. "Melling, even with a mask, I'd know that towhead of yours anywhere. Your mother would skin you alive if she knew what you were doing."

"But my father would be pleased."

The bigger one knocked him upside the head. "Go on, Alex!"

The blond took off running—two more following him.

"A bunch of babies!" Rupert cursed a few times then shouldered past Josephine's rescuer. "You ain't nothing special. You wouldn't even be on this street if your uncle didn't take you in."

"And you'll never amount to anything if you don't learn to treat others with respect."

As soon as the last boy sauntered off, the young man knelt beside Josephine.

"You poor thing." He gently wiped his thumb across her cheek to clear the yolk. "Did you mean to be an egg sand-*witch* tonight?"

She couldn't help but smile at his grinning face.

"Up you go, darling."

He kept hold of one of her hands once she stood, but she couldn't form words to declare her undying devotion.

"Where do you live?"

Josephine shuffled down the driveway, looking at the nearby houses to gauge her location before pointing to the left.

"Allow me to walk you home." He picked the crumpled witch's hat off the ground and motioned to the right. "Do you know that big two-story across the way? That's where I live—the Finnigans' house. Remember that. Come to me if those boys ever bother you. Ask for me or Althea, the kitchen girl. She'll pass word if I'm not home."

Too awed to ask his name, she nodded.

"Why did those rascals pick on you? Do you have a brother their age that they're upset with?"

Josephine shook her head. "I'm almost six and my brother is seven."

"They're a bunch of dunderheads. I've got a couple years on them and a decade on you, but I don't mind stepping up when help is needed."

"Thank you."

Closer to Washington Square Park, several costumed youngsters congregated near the streetlamps, staring at her humiliated state.

"Witchy Wolf!" Edgar yelled as he ran by, his red hair like a torch in the night.

Laughter followed them down Charles Street, but the young man never let go of Josephine's hand. She pointed to the house across from the park.

He stopped at the base of the front steps. "What's your name, little one?"

"Jo. Josephine Wolf."

"Do you need me to talk to your parents to explain things, Jo?"

"No!" She jerked away.

He squatted so he could look her in the eyes. The flickering porchlight made his stare golden. "Is there trouble at your house?"

Josephine nodded. "Mama is dying. Papa spends all his time with her when he isn't working. Mathias and I have to be quiet. Miss Sarah keeps an eye on us while she's cooking and cleaning, but Mat and I know how to behave."

"I'm sure you do." He patted her shoulder, not shying away from the mess on her cape. "You're brave, and having a brother and father with you is a blessing. I have a cousin and aunt at my uncle's house. I moved in with them after my parents died."

The front door opened, and Mathias's dark head peeked out.

"Take care of your sister," the rescuer said before handing Josephine her hat and walking away.

"What are you doing out here, Jo?" Mathias whispered. "And what happened to you?"

She climbed the five steps to the porch, passing under the gleaming white gingerbread trim their mother was proud of. "Some boys caught me in the yard and drug me two blocks away. That bigger boy saved me, but that was after I got egged."

"You weren't supposed to go outside after supper." He shook his head as she crossed the threshold, then switched to their silent speaking. *You're going to have to wash your clothes in the bathroom before anyone sees you.*

I know, Josephine replied.

Why didn't you call to me?

I was too scared.

He followed her to the mid-floor landing, making the ninety-degree turns on the open stairwell.

I could have told Papa, and he would have gone.

Stopping in the upstairs hall, Josephine shook her head and whispered. "Mama needs him more. Besides, God sent me a handsome prince."

"You're a ninny!"

Josephine shushed him.

"That wasn't a prince, that's Sean Spunner. He's on the boxing team at Spring Hill. Those other boys were probably scared of him."

Pleased to finally know her rescuer's name, Josephine tossed her cape and hat into the bathtub. "Most of them ran away as soon as he arrived."

"He's no magical prince, so don't rely on him. Call out to me, Jo. I might be your only hope next time."

But she was determined for there to never be a next time.

Two
1899

On November third, Josephine stood by her mother's headstone in Magnolia Cemetery, arms around the angel statue.

"If Papa finds out I skipped school midday to come here, I'll be in trouble." Josephine kissed the angel's cheek and settled cross-legged on the grass, tracing the date on the marker that showed Helen Wolf had passed away three years previous that very day. "Mathias knows where I am. He's supposed to meet me here after school."

Josephine visited the grave often, talking out her fears and enjoying the solitude outdoors without worries of the neighborhood boys like Edgar Melvin teasing her. Sean Spunner came around at least once a week, but with him out in Spring Hill for college, he couldn't stop all the teasing. Some threw things at "Witchy Wolf," others tried to trip her when she walked by at school or in the park. Even with Francesca and Sadie at her side, the taunts were relentless and taking their toll on her friendships. Sadie had started a private school that autumn and spent less time with Josephine and Francesca each week, preferring her new friends that weren't hounded by the local bully.

But that afternoon Josephine's mind was on her father.

"Mama," Josephine said with a sigh as she laid back in the grass and gazed at the azure sky, "I wish I knew Papa was okay. He's still so quiet and sad looking. Help me check on him. I've flown as far as home to here and back, but his office by the river is a lot further."

Her skinny arms settled beside her torso and she closed her eyes against the afternoon sun. "I know I can do it with your help, Mama."

As she'd done a dozen times when alone in her room at night, Josephine purposely relaxed her body and cleared her mind. Imagining she was floating, her spirit released its tether and rose from her prone body.

Josephine looked down at her messy brown braids, freckled nose, and the black stockings sticking out from under her checkered dress. She wasn't any different than her friends with the exception of the invisible stain of eggs from that Halloween night and the label of witch still mocking her.

Josephine's spirit stood on a nearby cross-shaped headstone. From there she jumped to another marker, hopping across the green expanse until she flew over the cemetery gates and into the air.

Six blocks north, she circled Washington Square Park. Glancing further east, Josephine caught the glimmer of water beyond the city. She'd never flown further than this, but she felt the pull to check on her father. Her family's home across from the park was always her starting point. Keeping to that, she perched on the second story, resting on the curving fretwork that framed the balcony. From there she could hear Miss Sarah singing as she went about her chores within the house.

Smiling over the comforting tune, Josephine took to the sky once more and followed Government Street so she wouldn't get lost. She'd only ever been downtown and to the riverfront with her father or Miss Sarah, and the city of Mobile looked different from the air. The oaks were smaller, the buildings not as intimidating. Except for the courthouse. Josephine went directly to the statue of Marianne, Goddess of Liberty, set among the spires of the majestic building at the corner of Royal and Government Streets. The woman looked even larger when

Josephine was on her level. Feeling a surge of power from the unseeing eyes, she curtseyed to the statue and flew across Royal Street to the top of the city hall complex to survey the riverfront.

The warehouses and buildings looked alike from above, but Josephine had a vivid memory of the time her father took her to see his office. She went to the shipping building and wound her way through the desks until she found her father hunched over a pile of papers. Statistics were his specialty. He could figure out the best way to do something and save the company money in the process, but he couldn't save his beloved wife from her consumptive illness. Josephine's mother was bedridden for all of the girl's memories, and she thought her mother must still be like that to her father, too, because he continued to live the same routine of work and home time.

Her father was pale with brown hair, like Josephine, but she hoped her hazel eyes weren't as sad as his, though they probably were. She stood across from him at the head of his desk, watching the way he studied the rows of numbers on the chart.

"Smile, Papa," she whispered. "I love you."

Brow furrowed, he looked up. Josephine would have sworn he looked right at her as the corner of his mouth twitched. Then he rubbed his face and stood.

She wanted to follow him down the hall but felt tired. She was miles away from her body and didn't know how much energy she needed to return. Taking the shortest way outside, she leapt into the air once more.

By the time she reached Washington Square, her vision blurred. Wishing she could fall into bed, she instead continued south of the neighborhood, dropping lower as she neared the cemetery.

Mathias knelt beside her body, patting her cheek and shaking her shoulder.

"Jo! Wake up, Jo! You can't be dead." He wiped at his nose with his sleeve.

Mathias lurched back at the mental words. Their silent connection had served them well during the years of their mother's illness, when they had to be quiet around the house while she rested, and they continued to use it. These days, Josephine would plead for Mathias to get help when she was outnumbered, but she still had to fight the other kids off until Mathias arrived.

When Josephine's spirit drifted into her body she immediately gasped, limbs twitching.

"Jo, you ninny!" Mathias scowled, a look he'd perfected during his ten years of life made all the more dangerous with his deep brown eyes. "I thought you were dead. Don't scare me like that."

"Sorry, I was…" She had yet to tell her brother about the spirit wanderings she had begun experimenting with the month before. Sharing their connection was one thing, but this felt more personal. "I was deep in my mind."

"Well, get up."

He tried to help her sit, but Josephine was too heavy in her physical body.

"I need a minute."

"But there's a ball game going on over near Tom's street and—"

"Go on, Mat. I can get back alone."

He shrugged. "Suit yourself. Call for me when Papa gets home."

Josephine slowly sat up and watched Mathias run down the gravel lane separating the lots within the sprawling cemetery. His black hair shone amid the white monuments.

"He looks like you, Mama. You had the prettiest raven hair and brown eyes. Thank you for helping me fly to Papa." She stood, legs wobbling. "I need to build up to longer adventures so I'm not as drained next time."

It took Josephine fifteen minutes to make it to the gates because she had to stop to rest after crossing each lot. Once on the street dotted with homes, her pace increased. The neighborhood meant predators, and she didn't want to be in their territory longer than needed. The six-block walk north was perilous enough on a day she could run.

When the edge of Washington Square Park finally came into view, the friendly faces of Francesca Wilton and Sadie Marley waited for her.

"Jo!" Francesca called.

The girls met her on the corner, and each threw an arm around her.

Rather than collapsing against them, their nearness strengthened Josephine. She stood taller and smiled as she hugged them, forgiving Sadie's recent slights in favor of her current support.

"Mathias told us you went to the cemetery," Sadie said with a toss of her blonde ponytail, "but I'm not allowed to go that far from home."

Francesca nodded in agreement, her brunette braid slipping over her shoulder. "We waited here for you."

"Thank you."

"Look, fellas, it's a gathering of witches." Edgar Melvin crossed Augusta Street with two cronies at his back.

"I'm not a witch!" Sadie snapped at the twelve-year-old who lived on her street. She sounded brave, but she inched behind Josephine.

"I guess you might not be, but Witchy Wolf and that big-nosed Franny Wilton sure are." Melvin stopped a few feet in front of them, mocking smile flashing in time with his friends' laughter.

"You take that back!" Josephine lunged at the boy, fists striking.

The surprise move enabled her to give him a bloody nose. Edgar bellowed like a wounded bull and knocked Josephine to her backside.

Sadie shrieked and ran through the park in retreat, drawing the attention of the lady in the yard across the street.

"Young man!" Mrs. Graves called as she hurried through the park. Merritt Graves had moved into the house opposite the park from Josephine the year after her mother died and had always been kind.

Edgar's attention being pulled to the adult allowed Josephine to kick him in the shin before struggling to her feet. As Mrs. Graves grew closer, Josephine tackled Edgar.

"Josephine Wolf, that's no way for a young lady to act!" Mrs. Graves admonished before turning to the instigator. "And there's no reason for a young man to pick on a girl, especially one younger and smaller. You should be ashamed of yourself. If I see behavior like this again, I'll tell each of your parents. Now all of you boys get on home."

Once the boys were leaving, the petite woman turned on Francesca. "Miss Wilton, I'm sure your mother would be horrified to know you witnessed a brawl in the park. Why don't you run home?"

Francesca nodded solemnly. "If Jo's all right, I will."

"I'm fine." Josephine gave a wicked grin. "But even if I wasn't, giving Edgar a bloody nose would make me better."

"He's gonna get you for that," Francesca whispered before leaving.

"Let him try. I'll send Sean Spunner after him."

Merritt Graves laughed. "Sean asked me to help keep an eye on you, but he's too big to be fighting kids."

Josephine brushed the backside of her dress. "Sean doesn't need to fight. He just looks at the boys with a mean glare and threatens to clobber anyone who messes with me."

"Obviously that doesn't work," Mrs. Graves said with a smile.

"It does when he's on break from school, but thank you for coming over, Miss Merritt."

"You're welcome, Josephine. Now get home."

"And you. Where's your baby?"

"She's on the porch with Aunt Ethel and Tippet guarding her." Merritt smiled. "Come over and see us sometime."

"I will, Miss Merritt."

As soon as Josephine was on her front porch, she turned to wave at Mrs. Graves, who she knew would still be watching her. The woman waved back and entered her gate on the opposite block.

Jo, I know I said you couldn't be dead this past hour, but I'm ready to strangle you! I now have a busted nose, compliments of Edgar.

The angry message from her brother caused Josephine to sink to the porch steps—once again weak from her adventures that afternoon.

I'm sorry, Mat, but he had it coming to him.

But I surely didn't! Being your brother isn't worth the suffering.

I'll make it up to you someday.

Three
1901

On July twelfth, Josephine and Francesca laid in the shade of the Wolfs' lawn, hoping a spare breeze would blow in from the Gulf. The heat—unnaturally dry and still—baked the girls at a time of day when they should have been enjoying an afternoon thunderstorm from the porch.

"If we were boys," Josephine lamented, "we could be with Mat and his friends at the creek, jumping off the rope swing and sticking our feet in the mud to cool off even quicker."

Francesca shuddered. "Not the mud—not since you found those crawdads at the bottom of the creek last year."

"You can't let little things like crawdads scare you, Fran. We could strip down to our underclothes and jump right in."

"But Miss Sarah said we weren't to follow Mathias today."

"That's because she heard him talking about skinny dipping. She doesn't want us to see the boys like that—says we're all getting too old, but we don't have anything up top yet so we're still just like the boys if everyone keeps their drawers on." Josephine pulled her dress above her bare legs and fanned herself with the skirt.

The screen door to the house snapped shut, and Miss Sarah's heavy steps crossed the porch. "Miss Jo, you better put that dress down. Just because the thermometer says it's 102 doesn't mean the whole of Washington Square needs to see you've got a rip on your ruffled drawers from climbing trees before breakfast."

Francesca giggled as Josephine huffed her annoyance while sitting up. "It's too hot, Miss Sarah."

"Then go inside for a bath and a nap, Miss Jo." The housekeeper looked at Francesca. "And I'm sure Mrs. Wilton would agree with that for you as well."

"I'm going to climb a tree again to see if I can't catch a breeze." Josephine stood and held out a hand to pull her friend upright. "Come on, Fran."

Crossing the street felt like journeying a desert in the uncanny heat. Francesca stood at the base of one of the twisting live oaks and watched Josephine hoist herself up a dozen feet.

"Come on, Fran. This is the easiest tree on the block."

"My mamma would kill me if I ripped my stockings." She motioned to her black clad legs.

17

"And your mamma will kill *you* forcing those abominations on you on a day like this."

Francesca dabbed her handkerchief across her brow. "I think I will go home and lie in the bath for an hour. It's the only way I'll get these stockings off before bed."

"Want to catch lightning bugs this evening?" Josephine asked before her friend could walk away.

"Maybe, but if it doesn't cool off, I'd rather stay home and read under the electric fan."

Josephine shrugged and gave a smile. "I'll see you later, Fran."

As she watched her friend leave, a growing sense of isolation crept over Josephine on her perch. She should return home, but even the thought of crossing the street alone washed her with dread. Perhaps she could stay hidden in her lofty perch until Mathias returned.

When Francesca reached Chatham Street, Edgar Melvin came around the corner beside Miss Merritt's house. There were no friends with him, but that didn't stop him from harassing Francesca.

"Where's your witchy friend, big-nosed Franny?"

Josephine immediately climbed down. She feared for herself, but bravery came easily enough when her friends were involved.

"You leave her alone!" Josephine stopped arm's length away from Edgar. "If you had any brains in your head, you'd see Francesca's nose is in perfect proportion to her face."

"To go with her big, ugly mouth and head?"

Josephine leapt at the thirteen-year-old, fingers scratching at his face with enraged blows. Edgar's hands went around her neck, but she kept her arms flying as he lowered her to the sidewalk with his overpowering grip. Her vision clouded but she heard a horse approach. The stomp of hooves and the equestrian odor that went with it filled her remaining senses.

"Get your hands off her!" Sean Spunner commanded as booted feet struck the earth nearby.

Edgar's hands released, but Josephine kept blindly striking until she touched nothing and heard him running away. Then her arms fell limp at her sides.

"Can you not take the hottest day of the year off from fighting, Jo Wolf?" Sean asked as he fanned her with his straw hat.

Josephine opened her eyes and looked up at the kneeling figure, a flutter squirming in her middle. "I'll never stand by when one of my friends is insulted."

"Jo should have been born in the age of knights, don't you think Miss Wilton?" Sean asked with a grin.

"She would have been burned at the stake," Francesca replied with a sardonic tone.

Sean laughed, replaced his hat, and scooped Josephine into his arms as he stood. "Would you please lead Heathcliff into Merritt's yard, Miss Wilton? Don't worry about his size. He's gentle."

"Yes, Mr. Spunner," Francesca hesitantly reached for the reins of the brown stallion standing placidly on the side of the road. "Should I leave the gate open for you to follow?"

Sean held Josephine's gaze as he cradled her in his arms. "Do you wish for me to carry you home or do you want to stop in Merri's house before running off to find more trouble?"

"Neither. I'm going to visit my mother."

"In this heat, darling? You'll burn to a crisp in the middle of that plot. Why, you don't even have a hat."

"Then loan me yours."

He laughed, amber eyes bright under the sheen on his shaded brow.

"I guess I don't need it to visit Ethelwynne." Sean loved Merritt's two-year-old daughter, visiting her more often than he checked on Josephine. If the Graves family wasn't so kind, Josephine would have been jealous of his attentions to them. "I can't in good conscience let you go off alone after you were attacked—not to mention the heat. Allow me to escort you to the cemetery gates."

Josephine looked at her friend standing awkwardly with the horse. "And see Fran to George Street."

"She's demanding, isn't she, Miss Wilton?" Sean asked with a wink, causing Francesca to giggle.

"I'll do anything to protect my friends," Josephine declared.

"Come on, Jo. Hold on to Heathcliff's mane." Sean lifted her to the saddle and gently took the reins from Francesca, who he then offered his arm to. "We'll see you to George Street, Miss Wilton."

Once Francesca was safely in her one-story house, Sean swung into the saddle behind Josephine. His hands were on the reins, but Josephine focused on his muscular thighs nestled around her legs and his hot torso against her back.

"Hang on, darling."

The wind was just as hot as the air, but riding with Sean was exhilarating, even at the slow trot. Josephine imagined holding his hand and showing him how she flew—above the buildings and skimming treetops in her spirit wanderings.

At the cemetery gates, Sean kept going. "Allow me take you all the way in, Jo."

She nodded and relaxed against him as they cantered down the narrow dirt lanes. As soon as the horse stopped, Josephine swung her leg over and slipped to the ground. Without speaking, Sean dropped his wide-brim hat onto her head.

Gazing up at her hero, she grinned as big as his smile. "I'll bring it back to you, Sean."

"I know you will. Take care of yourself, darling." He turned his horse around and respectfully headed for the nearest gate.

Josephine immediately kissed her mother's marker, settled on the grass in the slim shade of the angel statue, and reclined with Sean's hat over her face. Breathing in the smell of his aftershave and sweat, she released her physical tethers and flew after him.

Sean went directly to Merritt's house. He saw that Heathcliff was comfortable with water and a quick rubdown in the stable and then joined Merritt and little Ethelwynne on the grass beneath the satsuma trees strung with colorful bottles. He played with the child by covering his face with his hands and then making silly faces at her.

Once last year, Josephine asked Merritt about Sean's relationship with them. Merritt admitted that he had been in love with her younger cousin but she'd passed away from yellow fever in 1897. Still reeling from the loss of his wife the year before, Mr. Wolf had sent his children to stay with their grandparents when that epidemic struck the city, but Josephine remembered seeing Sean in the yard with the pretty fifteen-year-old that summer before she was sent away.

Are you of the living or of the dead, child? a wavering voice asked within her mind.

Josephine jerked on the clothesline where she perched and looked about. Sean, Merritt, and Ethelwynne carried on as though nothing had changed.

You shouldn't go wandering when your body is unprotected.

Oh! Josephine jumped into the air and traveled as fast as she could back to Magnolia Cemetery.

Standing over her prone body was a stooped woman in a sky blue dress with white hair braided around the crown of her head. Her wrinkled face was stern and her hands were clasped around an old parasol handle that shaded her with its faded black lace and silk canopy.

What are you waiting for, child?

How can you talk to me in your head?

It takes a lot of effort at my age, so I'd appreciate it if you'd get back in your body.

Josephine quickly settled her spirit and physically sat upright, removing the hat from her head as she did so. Eyes wide, she met the stare of the old woman who looked down on her. The wrinkled face cracked further with smile lines.

"If those aren't the eyes of mischief, I don't know what is," the woman said.

"Why do you say that, ma'am?" Josephine asked as she stood.

"The eyes are the windows to the soul, child, and yours twinkle with joy, pain, and intelligence." The woman's brown eyes bore into Josephine's heart. "Who taught you to astral project?"

"To astral…oh, you mean spirit wander. No one."

"And your telepathy—mind talk?"

"I figured it out when I was four and taught my brother. He's the only one who's spoken to me like that before." She lowered her head, embarrassed to admit her next words. "You startled me when you did it."

The woman's thin hands were cool and paper soft as she skimmed Josephine's cheek. "Child, you are a wonder, but you need instruction."

"Would you teach me?" Josephine bounced with excitement.

"I've been waiting decades for someone with your intuitive intellect and spark. What's your name, child?"

"Jo—Josephine—Wolf. And yours?"

"Mrs. Rettig. I live just beyond the western cemetery gate and have a garden I could use help tending."

"I'm a good worker." Josephine eagerly smiled.

A gnarled finger pointed to the inscription at the base of the angel. "Is that your mother, Jo Wolf?"

She nodded, shoulders slumping. "This is my safe spot. I feel peace when I'm here with her."

Mrs. Rettig smiled knowingly. "Come with me, child. There is much for you to learn."

Josephine reverently cradled the thin hand in hers and matched the woman's steady pace. Beneath the small shadow the parasol created, they crossed Ann Street. At the faded, sagging house beyond a massive oak, Mrs. Rettig led Josephine to the kitchen.

The woman pointed to the table and chairs. "You need refreshment first. Astral traveling is tiring, even if you don't realize it. Be sure to drink before and after, and never go far on an empty stomach."

"Yes, ma'am."

Josephine sat primly at the table and watched the hostess retrieve two empty canning jars from a cabinet. Mrs. Rettig collected a pitcher of opaque liquid from the icebox and poured it into the jars. When one was set before her, Josephine studied the flecks of green that floated to the top.

"It's lemonade, child."

"I've never seen lemonade that looks like this."

"Lemons are expensive. I make it with lemon balm and mint from my garden."

Josephine took a sip, then a longer drink to feel the cooling tingle on her tongue. "It's wonderful!"

"There is a lot you can do with herbs, just as there is a lot you can do with your mind. I'll teach you how to use the powers of nature for the benefit of others. It's your destiny to heal and bring peace." Mrs. Rettig patted her hand. "But you must master your impulse to lash out. I see it in the mischief burning in your eyes."

"Even if it's against evil and injustice?"

Mrs. Rettig's thin lips broke into a smile. "I won't teach you to judge another, but I trust you'll find balance."

After drinking, they went into the yard crowded with plants. It lacked official garden borders, but each section was neatly planted within its space. Mrs. Rettig named every shrub, flower, and herb as Josephine pulled weeds from around them. Lavender, rosemary, thyme. Josephine caressed the velvety petal of the white sage and listened to the old woman's claims of how it could benefit a home by burning it to cleanse the air.

An hour later, Mrs. Rettig made Josephine retreat to the shade of the magnolia and brought her another glass of lemonade.

"After you've rested, go home," she told Josephine, "If you wish to return, light a candle under tonight's new moon sky to invite this education into your life."

"I will, ma'am," Josephine promised. "I want to know everything."

The rest of that summer, Josephine spent hours every morning with Mrs. Rettig. She weeded and pruned and listened to the woman share her knowledge. Once school started back in the autumn, Josephine stopped in every afternoon, sometimes with a reluctant Francesca in tow. The garden looked better than it had in a decade and Josephine's knowledge and abilities grew even faster than her maturing body over the next few years.

Four
1905

When the floral parade ended, Josephine and Francesca and their new friend, Cordelia Barnes, left downtown to return to Washington Square. They were pleased for the warm day that allowed them to forgo coats and better show off their corseted shapes beneath their pink ruffles.

"Is Mardi Gras season always so exciting?" Cordelia asked. Having moved to town from the south county over the holidays, she was full of wonder over the city's Carnival and the attentions Josephine collected from boys of all ages.

"Typically," Francesca replied. "Jo and I have been going to all the parades since we were five. I'm glad we're now old enough to go without a parent tagging along."

"So long as we don't speak to rowdy boys," Josephine said in a perfect mimic of Francesca's mother.

"But the rowdy boys are always talking to Jo," Cordelia said with a smirk.

"But not for the best reasons," Francesca said with a roll of her eyes. "You're getting too old to get into fist fights, Jo."

"Then tell the boys to leave me alone because I'll always defend myself and my friends." Josephine stopped to admire a lone azalea bloom on a sun-drenched bush. "Have you ever seen this shade of pink, Del?"

Cordelia leaned closer. "No, I don't think so. I wonder if it's confused because the others aren't opened. Do you mind if I pluck it so I can take it home and try to mix my watercolors to get this shade?"

Smiling with importance, Josephine was proud her friend looked to her for guidance on respecting living things. From Mrs. Rettig she had learned to cultivate plants so that they might help people and respected animals so much she did not eat the ones who roamed the lands or flew in the sky like she did with her spirit. Fortunately, her father and Miss Sarah respected her choices, giving her space in the yard to garden and appropriate meals to keep healthy.

"I think it would be a worthy sacrifice, Del. Be sure to press it in your Bible and keep it always." They started back on the walk. "Now who is going to go to the cemetery with me? I'll be stopping at Mrs. Rettig's afterward."

"I promised Mother I'd return straight home after the parade," Francesca said, though Josephine knew she'd have a valid excuse because she avoided the cemetery like yellow fever. "I need to do that so when I ask about going out Saturday, she'll say yes without questions."

"I will!" Cordelia said. "My mother wanted us to help clear the dead vegetation from the back yard, but that's something my brothers could do. Besides, they like burning the stuff afterward."

"I'll be sure to warn my mother so she closes our windows."

"Ever the dutiful daughter, Fran. At least as far as your mother knows," Josephine joked because Francesca was always up for a bit of naughtiness—so long as it didn't involve gravestones.

When the friends arrived on George Street, Mrs. Barnes was sweeping her front porch.

"There you are, Cordelia. Your brothers returned fifteen minutes ago."

"It's not my fault they like to run."

"Say goodbye to your friends and change into your work clothes."

"But I was going to go with Jo to the cemetery."

"Another day, dear. Your brothers need your help."

Josephine said farewell to her friends. Cordelia went into the house on the left, Francesca the one on the right. They were lucky to live next door to each other, but Josephine was glad only a few blocks separated them from her.

On her way to Magnolia Cemetery, she felt the prickles of someone following. Refusing to turn around, she instead called to her brother.

Mathias, where are you?

On my way home.

Where? I need you.

What for? You've been staying out of trouble lately.

As far as you know, maybe. I'm crossing Selma, on my way to visit Mama. Someone is following me, but I don't want to look.

Loop back and go home.

She increased her pace out of spite. *I want to see Mama, and I promised Mrs. Rettig I'd visit this afternoon.*

Unless you're working a new power, you can't see Mama. And that old lady can do without you for a day.

Thanks for nothing. I'll deal with the threat myself. Since you're privy to my agenda, you know where to look for the body.

Don't be morbid. You might not even be in danger.

Who said it would be my *body?*

Very funny, Jo. I'm just crossing Broad Street.

Forget it. I'll see you at home later.

No longer concentrating on the conversation, Josephine strained to hear any sounds that might accompany the burning stare. Footsteps in the road. She had to know what she was up against. At the next block, Josephine paused and turned abruptly. The leering stare of Edgar Melvin walking two house lengths behind gave her goosebumps.

When an automobile horn honked, she jumped.

"Little Miss Josephine," Sean Spunner said as he pulled to a stop. His grin was the same as when he had first rescued her nearly a decade before, save for a small chip on one of his front teeth. "Aren't you pretty in pink, darling! Did you attend the floral parade?"

"Yes," she said as she placed a hand on his shining automobile. "And now I'm going to visit my mother."

Sean looked down the road and leaned closer. "Do you have a suitor hoping to rendezvous with you in the privacy there?"

"No, he's a red-headed horror and has been following me."

"Then allow me to escort you to Magnolia Cemetery." Sean hurried around to open the door, then pulled a scarf out of the glovebox for Josephine to tie over her hair. She held it instead.

Once they were on their way, she changed her plans in case Edgar still followed. "Would you bring me to Mrs. Rettig's house instead? She lives west of—"

"Everyone knows where Old Lady Rettig lives," Sean said with a grin. "Aren't you a little young to need something from her?"

"Need? She's been teaching me about herbs for years now." She met his glance with a questioning gaze. "How did you chip your tooth?"

"In the boxing ring. Freddy Davenport took advantage when my guard was down."

"I like it. Thank him for me."

Sean laughed. "You still have plenty of spunk, Jo Wolf, though it's been a while since I've heard any stories of you besting one of the boys."

"I'll have to increase my efforts then." She motioned to the oak tree in front of the little house. "Here is fine, thank you."

He came around to open her door. "I'm still happy to help, even if I'm busy at the office or in court most days."

"The law profession is better off for your efforts, I'm sure. Thank you for the ride, Sean."

She offered her hand to shake his, but he kissed the back of it instead, causing a quiver in her middle.

"Anytime, Jo. Take care of yourself." He winked.

Smiling, Josephine let herself in Mrs. Rettig's front door as she always did. The woman looked exhausted in her rocking chair by the front window, knotted hands clasped in her lap.

"Josephine, I'm glad you came. Come sit with me," her voice croaked.

Smile fading, Josephine went right to her side and cupped the woman's wrinkled cheeks in her hands. "Mrs. Rettig, what can I do to help today?"

"Sit with me, as I said. There is much to tell you."

Josephine perched on a stool at the woman's knee, eyes intense as she felt the change of energy from her friend.

"I want you to take my books home with you today and keep them."

She glanced at the three ancient tomes proudly displayed on the mantel covering plants, spiritual energy, and healing. "But you love your books."

"My eyes are failing, Josephine. There's no reason for me to keep them only to pet when you could learn from them. It will help me rest easier knowing they're with someone who cares."

"I care, Mrs. Rettig."

"I know you do. And dig out your favorite plants from the garden." A knobby finger pointed toward the rear of the house. "Take that wagon by the back porch and fill it. I know you have seedlings from all my plants, but there's no sense in these going to brambles when there's someone capable to care for them."

"But—"

"I'm dying, Josephine. Eighty-two years is nothing to be ashamed of, and the fact that you know my most important skills allows me to rest easier."

"But that means there's more you've never taught me."

She nodded, her silvery hair a dull shade of death. "The rest is in the books should you need them. Go on and fill the wagon."

Josephine trudged outside, stopping to tie on an apron that was hanging on the back porch. Miss Sarah would fuss at her for gardening in her good clothes, but she had to follow Mrs. Rettig's wishes.

Mat? I do need you after all. She said while she dug around a white sage bush.

I figured as much. I'm sitting with Mama's angel.

Josephine smiled. *She'll like that. I'm at Mrs. Rettig's house and need your help getting home. Come around to the back yard.*

Mathias grumbled, but Josephine knew he would arrive in a few minutes. She had the wagon ready when he ambled around the corner. He'd grown tall and handsome—all her friends said so. His athletic build and skills on the baseball field were noteworthy, his dark coloring striking thanks to their mother's Greek heritage. With his linen trousers and crisp white shirt, he could have been mistaken for a college boy rather than a pupil at Barton Academy.

You're going to owe me for being seen at the witch's hut. This is the last time I'm coming here.

Yes, it'll be the last time.

Mathias lifted her lowered chin, seeing the finality in his sister's eyes. "I'm sorry, Jo."

She shrugged. "Everyone I love dies eventually. If you can get the wagon, I'll collect the books and say goodbye."

Five
1912

It was the first Friday in December, and Josephine's twenty-second birthday was in ten days. Determined to change her life's projection by that milestone date, she took inspiration from her father who had finally rid himself of over fifteen years of mourning. Mr. Wolf was courting a lady with barely a decade on his children. Josephine and Mathias both feared the match— not for their father's sake, but for their own. Mathias was determined to move out before a new wife moved in, and Josephine was beyond ready to open her life to lovers and new experiences.

Without the freedom of a young man earning his own living, Josephine was nearly helpless in her living situation. Her herb garden provided a small income, but she felt her lack of experience was something she could change. She was ready to become a woman of the world because even if she was forever branded the Witchy Wolf of Washington Square, she didn't want to be a virginal spinster, too.

Downstairs, Sarah Bryant, the Wolfs' long-time housekeeper, had the dining room filled with the aroma of biscuits and coffee.

"Good morning, Miss Sarah," Josephine called through the doorway to the kitchen as she took her seat at the table. "Have you seen my cat?"

"Morning, Miss Jo," her husky voice replied. "I let Midnight out already."

"Thank you. He ran down before I was dressed." Pouring a cup of coffee, she eyed the newspaper folded beside her father's chair at the head of the table and her brother's empty space across from hers.

"You're the early bird today." Sarah hurried in from the kitchen with a tray of food. She placed the covered dishes in the middle of the setting, then smoothed back her frizzy brown hair.

"It's not surprising since Mat didn't stumble in until after two in the morning."

"The rascal. And we have a big day with Miss Jensen coming for supper."

Josephine sighed at the reminder, knowing her father planned to propose that night. She used to think he should marry Sarah and those feelings had been renewed recently because the housekeeper's comforting form would be appreciated more than the strangeness of Marlene Jensen.

After helping herself to an orange and a few cheese slices, Josephine looked at Sarah. "I think Mat drank to forget. I wish I had the option of rabble-rousing to let off steam."

"Now Miss Jo," Sarah said while concealing a smile, "you and Mathias are old enough to be pleased for your father. He deserves a happily ever after as much as anyone."

"But why Miss Jensen? She's an established society spinster with her own money. There's no need for either of them to break that respectable station by thrusting marriage to a widower with grown children into the mix."

Sarah laughed. "Ever heard of a thing called love, Miss Jo? It's still alive and well in this age, even if some of the young men are crass and women are seeking the right to vote."

Josephine rolled her eyes and pried apart the orange.

"If it bothers you too much, find yourself a match. Mathias is established enough in the accounting department at Hammel's to settle down with a family of his own, too."

Keeping quiet about her brother's plan to leave home—but not with a wife—she bit into a slice of orange.

Mr. Wolf entered the dining room with a pleased smile beneath his waxed mustache. "Good morning, Josephine." He kissed her forehead before taking his seat. "Are you doing well today?"

"Yes, thank you."

"Remember, supper tonight is formal. I expect you in the parlor at seven."

"Is this really such a good idea, Papa? We aren't used to entertaining."

"I know you aren't the hostess type, Jo, but if all goes well, a new lady will be able to fill that role for our house. All I ask is for you to be present and polite."

Mathias laughed as he came in. "Witchy Wolf can be anything but polite. Don't you remember how she used to tear into bullies?"

Mr. Wolf shook his head.

The only thing he remembered from those years was a raw ache in his chest. It was Miss Sarah who saw to Josephine's scrapes from schoolyard altercations, and Mathias who endeavored to defend his little sister against the growing instances of name-calling within the neighborhood. By the time she turned sixteen, no boys came within touching distance. Josephine had caused too many scratches, bruised shins, and other minor injuries for her tormentors to risk further retaliation.

"Well," Mathias said as he leaned back in his chair, "I'll do my best to straighten our girl out, but she has a mind of her own, Father."

"You both do, Mat, and I'm proud of that." He grinned at his son. "Seven o'clock sharp, in tails."

"Yes, sir."

Mr. Wolf and Mathias ate their biscuits, sausage, and gravy while Josephine picked apart a second orange. She waited until their father left for work to prod Mathias.

"You're going to show up, aren't you?"

"For supper, of course. It's just one meal. But you may be sure I'll be long gone from here before anyone says 'I do.'"

"Do you have prospects in case they make a short engagement?"

He nodded. "I'm looking at a place today on St. Francis Street. How would you like to tour it with me?"

"Where and when shall I meet you?"

"The Cawthon Hotel at noon for dinner. It's two blocks from there."

"That sounds nice."

Mathias wiped his mouth with the linen napkin, then kissed her cheek with distraction more than affection. Josephine finished her coffee.

"I'm going for a walk, Miss Sarah," Josephine said when Sarah came to retrieve the breakfast dishes. "And I'll be meeting Mat downtown for dinner."

"I'm glad you're getting out, Miss Jo."

"Because it will keep me occupied while you prepare for supper?"

"You know better than that," she quipped. "Don't forget a wrap. It's December, after all."

Pages on the calendar meant nothing to weather along the Gulf Coast, but Josephine retrieved her black capelet and felt derby from the hall tree. She crossed the road and took the sidewalk around Washington Square, dreaming of a man who would shower her with affections.

When there was a meow behind her, Josephine paused to scratch the back of Midnight's head. His glossy black coat always looked radiant in the sun, and his large, green eyes peered into her soul.

"Come along with me, Middy. And ignore the squirrels today. They only agitate you."

The cat followed behind her, tail in the air. They reached the Palmetto Street side of the park at the same time a gentleman crossed from the block east.

"Miss Wolf, is that you?"

Her long-ago prince had returned in the garb of a bachelor lawyer, still grinning as brightly as he had a decade ago.

"Yes, and good morning, Mr. Spunner."

He took her hand, kissing the back of it as he studied her face. "That black capelet gave me a vision of little Witchy Wolf all those Halloweens ago."

"Crying and covered in eggs?"

"You are forever the best egg sand-witch I've ever met." He bit his lip while his eyes roamed her figure. "You're still Miss Wolf, are you not? I haven't spoken to you in a few years."

"Yes, Mr. Spunner."

"Please call me Sean." Her cat rubbed against his legs and cried for attention, to which he obliged. "You can't be a proper witch without one of these about, can you, Miss Wolf? Are you headed somewhere I could accompany you?"

"Just for a walk. And call me Jo. Anyone who's seen me dripping with raw eggs has that right. I never ate them after that experience."

"You poor darling." He kissed her hand once more. "I'm coming from breakfast at my uncle's house. It was such a fine morning I walked over. I have my own house on Rapier. Half a dozen streets between us seems to have prevented me from running across you these past years."

Josephine nodded, knowing he'd established his own house a few months after he'd given her a ride to Mrs. Rettig's house over seven years ago. He was engaged the summer of that exchange, but his fiancée had an accident the following winter and he'd been alone all that time. She knew he wasn't attached to anyone because she often flew by his house at night to check on him while her body was lying in bed. She'd gotten stronger with her astral projection in the years since she'd developed the skill, and now she was able to spend hours outside her body at night and go so far as across Mobile Bay, but Sean's house and the cemetery were her favorite places to explore. When Sean was home, he was typically alone in his library. He never shut his curtains on that room, allowing her to watch him read for pleasure in his favorite chair or work on a case at the desk.

"I'd be pleased to walk with you now, Sean."

"That wouldn't put you too far out of your way?"

"I have nowhere to be until I meet my brother at the Vineyard Café at noon."

"Perhaps you could ride downtown with me when I go to the office."

When the stars aligned, they did so with speed and purpose! she thought. "Allow me to collect my purse and return Midnight to the house, if you don't mind."

He bowed and offered his arm in a flamboyant gesture. At the house, Josephine carried Midnight inside, dashed up the stairs to collect her bag, and rushed back down.

"I'm off until this afternoon, Miss Sarah!" she called, slamming out the front door.

She ran down the porch steps to where Sean waited by the oak tree.

Grinning at her, he fingered the dimples that sat like crescent moons on the upper corner of her lips. "You're still that girl, Jo—a starry-eyed witch with magic in her hazel eyes."

"Why did you stop checking on me? I adored your weekly greetings."

"I knew you could look after yourself. And when you turned eighteen, you didn't need me poking about. How many beaus have you had?"

Josephine laughed. "The Witchy Wolf of Washington Square? How many indeed, Sean Spunner! You're the only boy to do so much as hold my hand."

She expected him to joke, but his face was solemn. He stopped to stare.

"Josephine Wolf, the men in this town must be daft! Surely they've outgrown such name-calling by now."

"Outgrown, possibly. Forgotten, never. I don't think it helps that I grow herbs and sell them to midwives." She dropped his arm and continued down the sidewalk, crossing the next block alone.

"Jo, I feel the need to apologize for the idiocy of men." He caught up to her in front of Merritt Graves's house and re-offered his arm. "I can understand boys in their youth being obtuse, but men beyond university age should know better."

"Know better about what? I was never officially presented in society because I lack a mother to remind my father of the importance of such things as debut seasons."

"Have you been to a masquerade?"

In the dappled morning light, his eyes were as golden as she remembered them. She held his gaze, relishing his sincere concern, and shook her head.

"That will change this New Year's Eve, darling. I'll see that you receive an invitation to the Order of Mayhem's ball. Would your father escort you?"

"He's going to propose tonight. I doubt he'd want to leave behind his fiancée—if she accepts."

"I heard from my cousin that he's been courting Marlene Jensen. I often wonder why someone hadn't caught her before now."

"She's about your age," Josephine countered. "Why didn't you?"

"I prefer to have several years above a woman to put me on a more equal standing with her because of my youthfulness." Sean winked, his chipped front tooth flashing boyishly.

Josephine laughed, trying not to allow the indulgent thought that he might be thinking of her as a possibility. "You're ready to settle?"

"I have been for a while. I tried once before, but God had other plans." His steps slowed as they approached Rapier Street. "Do you want to rush into town, or would you want to come inside first?"

Her world was ready to implode, and Josephine figured she might as well go down like a shooting star. "I'd like to visit with you, Sean."

He discreetly looked up and down the street as they crossed. She wondered how bold it was to walk into a man's house without a chaperone. At least it was daylight. With the door opened to his tasteful foursquare home, Sean motioned her in.

"Your cape and hat, Witchy Wolf," he said as soon as the door closed.

Josephine handed him the black capelet, hat, and wrist bag. Her white shirtwaist and black skirt felt decidedly plain, but the way he looked her over was empowering.

"I don't suppose you'd like a drink?" he asked as he gently took her elbow. She shook her head. "Aunt Cecilia raves about your tea blends. She loves the autumn one you made these past few months. She used the rest with her breakfast today."

"She sends her cook to me to make regular purchases."

"I'm glad she appreciates your efforts, Jo. Would you like a tour of the house?"

"That isn't necessary. I'd like to talk."

"Do you mind the library? It's my favorite room."

She shook her head, and he guided her into a space rich with bookcases and leather seats she had observed from the window a hundred times.

They settled on either end of the chaise. Josephine boldly turned to him so their knees almost touched. "I turn twenty-two on the sixteenth."

"Happy early birthday, Jo. Has it truly been so long? I still see freckles on your nose."

"You've always been a gentleman to me, Sean, and I respect you immensely. There's something I need, and I know I can trust you."

"I'm as discreet as they come. Do you seek legal assistance?" He leaned closer, breath brushing her cheek with his words.

Josephine shook her head and gave a shy smile. "Some part of me knows you won't be shocked, though what I'm about to say defies polite society. I've never been courted and have no immediate prospects, but I'm brimming with passion. I want to be thoroughly kissed. And more."

"More?" Sean's bright eyes widened.

"Yes, so much more. Would you show me, Sean?" She took his hand. "I don't mean to spring this on you or sound desperate, but meeting you this morning was serendipitous, just as the night you first rescued me. Our age difference isn't a hindrance now, is it?"

He leaned closer and raised his free hand to cup her cheek. "Darling, you're bewitching. Look at any man the way you are me right now, and he would be yours. Open heart, vulnerable—it's too much to resist."

Sean's face came closer. Josephine would have flinched away, unsure what to do, but his hand cupping her face was joined by his other arm going around her waist as he tugged her closer. He was strong and hot, causing her to melt into his embrace as their lips fused. Her body understood what to do as it responded to Sean's caressing hands with similar movements around his back and shoulders. His lips traveled to her neck and he tongued below her ear. Electricity bloomed across her skin like a lightning strike.

"You're fire, Jo, so sweet and pliant." He pulled her against his firm chest.

"If you want more from me, I'd give it," she whispered.

He bestowed a kiss that included his tongue sensually sweeping into her mouth as he laid her the length of the chaise. The feel of his body nearly brought tears to her eyes with the intensity of it.

"You offer me a glorious gift, Jo." He pulled back. Gazing down at her, Josephine felt his wonder, but saw the sadness in his soul. "I respect you too much to take advantage at this moment. You experienced the kiss, but please think further about what you truly want. We'll revisit this subject later, I promise."

"Tonight?" She raised her brow as she took his offered hand.

He laughed as he pulled her upright. "I have a party to attend, and you have an important family evening. I'll stop by tomorrow. You can show me your garden, and we'll discuss things further."

"Ten in the morning?"

"How about eleven in case we both have a late night?"

Josephine nodded and looked at the rug. "I'll go now. Don't worry about bringing me downtown."

"Darling, don't be sad." Sean settled closer to her on the seat. "You're everything an intelligent man could want."

"But not you."

"That's where you're wrong, Jo. My desire is stirred. I'm restraining myself so neither of us regret what we both think we want to happen." He caressed his fingers through hers. "You know how sex works, don't you?"

She nodded, holding his stare.

"Then feel this so you know how appealing you are." His hand guided hers to his groin and Josephine's fingers trailed the length of his manhood. "The body doesn't lie, and neither do I. You deserve to be treasured when your time comes, Josephine Wolf."

Her hand paused, but the force of life beneath continued to throb. Seeing he watched her mouth, Josephine's lips curved into a smile. He mirrored it with one of his own.

"It's been a long time for me, but I've learned restraint over the years," he said with his deep voice. "If I was ten years younger, there would have been no hesitation when you requested *more*."

"Thank you, Sean." Her lips went to his, and he allowed her to lead the kiss. She deepened it, tonguing the chip on his front tooth, and playfully squeezed his thigh before leaning away.

"Are you sure I can't drive you into the city?"

"No thank you. I need a walk to regroup my thoughts." She stood and he followed.

"Do you know where my office is on Dauphin Street across from Bienville Square?" After she nodded, he continued. "Will you stop in and let me know you're all right? I'll be there until twelve-thirty, when I walk to the Aethelwulf Club for dinner."

"I'll try." She went for the hall, but Sean reached around her to retrieve her outerwear.

"I'm glad I don't have court today. I'd be too distracted." He placed the capelet around her. "Am I doing the right thing by letting you go right now?"

Josephine straightened her hat and memorized the sight of him staring with want as she retrieved the gloves from her purse. "I suppose we'll find out tomorrow morning. Goodbye, Sean."

Six

After dawdling through the shopping district, Josephine reached the corner of Dauphin and Conception Streets at five minutes after twelve. She glanced longingly down the block south of the park at the "Finnigan and Spunner" sign before turning north. The Cawthon Hotel was an impressive sight standing well above the oaks in the square. After leaving her hat and capelet at the coat check, she took the elevator to the seventh floor Vineyard Café.

"There you are, Jo." Mathias captured her hand as soon as she was off the elevator. "I was going to send for the police in another ten minutes. You're never late."

"Sorry, I was distracted. It's a big day for all of us," she said as means of deflecting from what he might see if he looked too closely.

"Never mind that. I've brought along a friend I want you to meet."

She followed her brother through the square tables and around the fountain in the middle of the restaurant to a table overlooking the park.

"Here she is, Cyrus."

A man in his late twenties with dark blond hair sporting a straight side part, striking deep-set blue eyes, and a defined jawline stood from the table. His Newport collar was high, the bowtie an elaborate poof of blue that further brightened his eyes. If Josephine hadn't spent time in Sean Spunner's arms that morning, she would have swooned.

"Jo, this is Cyrus Harrington, Cyrus, my sister, Josephine Wolf."

"How do you do, Miss Wolf?" Cyrus offered his hand and raised her gloved one to his lips, kissing the back of it. "I've heard much about you."

"Have you? You're a complete surprise to me, Mr. Harrington." She took the beech wood chair her brother offered between the two other place settings and removed her gloves, not shying from the fact that her hands were work-hardened.

Play nice, Jo.

It's been months since you've communicated with me this way, Mat, so shut up.

"Cyrus is new in Mobile," Mathias said aloud. "He moved from Atlanta and is currently in residence here at the Cawthon until permanent lodgings can be found. We've been helping each other out on our real estate searches. We're even thinking about going half on something."

Josephine snapped the napkin open and placed it in her lap as a waiter came by with an iced tea pitcher. "Don't do that, gentlemen. It's the worst situation to have to juggle when you're ready to settle down. Whoever gets a beau first will have to either kick the other fellow out or leave him with the mortgage when he goes off into a honeymoon cottage."

Cyrus laughed. "Your brother was right, Miss Wolf. You are amusing."

She raised her glass of sweet tea to him in a mock toast.

The waiter arrived at Mathias's side. "Are you ready to order, sir?"

"Yes, thank you. Go first, Cyrus, then I'll order for me and my sister."

Josephine glanced at the menu and telepathically told Mathias what she wished for. It was a game they had played since childhood, when their father or Sarah asked Mathias's opinion on food, treats, or presents. Mr. Wolf was surprised Mathias always guessed correctly. All except once. Mathias was mad at Josephine right before her fourteenth birthday, so he said she wanted a doll when she desperately wanted a corset and hair ribbons.

"The lady will have lentil soup and garden salad." Mathias then ordered roast beef and greens for himself.

"And a bottle of red to share, please," Cyrus added. "Something French."

The waiter bowed and left.

"Do you dine here often, Josephine?" Cyrus asked.

"No. Why?"

"I wondered how Mathias knew what to order for you?"

"My sister has a very particular food palate."

"Just say it, Mat." Josephine turned to his friend. "I don't eat meat other than select types of seafood."

"How interesting." Cyrus held her gaze. "Since I've moved here, I've discovered I have an abhorrence to crawdads and oysters."

"Those are options I refuse as well."

"I knew you two would get along fabulously," Mathias said with a smile.

"So, Mr. Harrington," Josephine said in her politest voice, "what work do you do?"

"Design of multiple types. My father has an architectural firm in Atlanta, but I was more interested in furnishing the insides of the buildings and floral design. I have too many contrary opinions to the old ways and felt it best to start fresh in a new city. I'm already hired to work on a few of the Mardi Gras tableaus and floats in the coming months."

"You're a tradition-breaker?"

"When I see fit."

"I approve, Mr. Harrington. There's much in society that demands refreshing."

"Call me, Cyrus, Miss Wolf." He grinned, broadening his face with the pull of dimples and smile lines.

"And allow me to be Jo to you, Cyrus."

The bottle of wine arrived. Lifting his filled glass, Cyrus looked to Josephine and then Mathias. "To new acquaintances."

As she set down her glass, both men watched whatever was going on behind her. A moment later, a hand rested on Josephine's shoulder.

"Miss Wolf, please excuse my intrusion." Sean removed his hand and stood by her side. "I couldn't go to dinner until I checked on your welfare, but I see you are well looked-after."

"Yes, thank you, Mr. Spunner. I arrived tardily, but made it safely. You remember my brother, Mathias. This is his friend, Cyrus Harrington, who's new in town. Gentlemen, Sean Spunner. He knew I was headed into town and hoped I'd stop by his office."

"Mr. Wolf, it's good to see you." He took their hands in turn. "And welcome to Mobile, Mr. Harrington. I've heard you're the great hope of the Order of Mayhem leaders with your tableau design for New Year's Eve."

"I plan to see that hope fulfilled, Mr. Spunner."

Sean nodded with a grin. "I won't intrude any longer. Do enjoy Jo's company."

"Would you care to join us, Mr. Spunner?" Mathias asked.

Josephine's cheeks heated as they awaited Sean's reply.

"I have a dinner meeting at the club, but I do appreciate the offer. Perhaps another time. Good afternoon, Miss Wolf, gentlemen."

Josephine couldn't see him walk away because she faced the window, but the other two watched him.

What the hell was that about, Jo?

She gave a slight shrug.

Don't tell me your prince is back after all these years.

And don't tell me I don't have a chance with him.

"He seems like a man about town," Cyrus remarked. "What club is he referring to? A country club?"

"No," Josephine replied, "the Aethelwulf. It's an exclusive men's club on the north side of the square."

"How intriguing."

"Jo has been infatuated with Mr. Spunner since she was a girl," Mathias offered. "He once saved her from a group of boys that were harassing her."

"It was an assault!" Anger burbled from her voice as she stood. "Those boys were older and hit me with dozens of raw eggs. And that was after almost forcing me to lift my dress for their benefit."

"Jo!" The shock looked almost like fear in her brother's eyes. "You never told me all that."

Don't make light of situations you don't understand! "Please, excuse me."

Mathias and Cyrus went to their feet, but she left without looking at them.

While Josephine was hiding in the ladies' room, Mathias prodded again.

I'm sorry, Jo. Please don't stay mad.

Go to hell, Mat.

I've never seen Mr. Spunner look at you like that. And Cyrus is concerned.

Ignoring him, she wiped her face with a cold, damp cloth. Then Josephine returned to the table, conscious of the eyes in the dining room watching after her hasty flight.

"Welcome back, Jo." Mathis pulled out her chair. "I'm so sorry for your pains, both caused by me and others."

She replaced the napkin on her lap. "That's enough on that subject. We don't want Cyrus thinking all Mobilians are unsettled, even if it's true."

They both laughed.

Balance restored, the three ate and conversed without further issues.

At the coat check, Cyrus held Josephine's capelet open and brought it around her shoulders with precise attention. She placed her felt hat on and checked the mirror, meeting his blue gaze over her shoulder in the reflection.

"Classic is definitely your style, Jo." He placed his fedora smartly on his head and grinned. "Will you do me the honor of walking with me?"

She accepted his offered arm, and they followed Mathias around to St. Francis Street. Josephine couldn't help but compare Cyrus to Sean. Cyrus was taller, but lean. His arm never wavered, but it felt flimsy compared to the bulk of Sean's muscles from his time boxing. She had watched him earlier that year at one of the local tournaments. Sean wasn't the best, but he looked wonderful in the ring.

"You have a pleased smile, Jo," Mathias said when he stopped at the bottom of a flight of stairs leading to an iron lace porch. "I hope it's for the building."

"It's brick and tall. Like Cyrus, I prefer to judge a house by what it offers on the inside."

Mathias jangled a set of keys. "Then come up. We'll tour the main affair before seeing the dungeon apartment. This one is partially furnished."

The airy front room beyond the entry hall was inviting.

"It seems to have solid bones and a tasteful beginning with the furnishings. Am I right, Cyrus?"

"Quite right, Jo."

Josephine flipped back the capelet and spun her hat around a finger as she strode into the dining room. She rapped the table surrounded by eight chairs. "I do love maple."

Mathias laughed. "You sound like you're ready to move in instead of me."

"No, not me, and certainly not you. This has to be Cyrus's place if you take the building. You, brother, may have the basement apartment because this has to be his canvas."

Mathias groaned. "Why did I think bringing you here would be a good idea?"

"I approve of your decision to involve Jo," Cyrus said. "It's refreshing to be with someone who understands my thinking."

"Jo is too intuitive for her own good. It typically spooks people."

"I'm not spooked," Cyrus said. "I'm thrilled with Jo's keen mind."

After seeing the functional kitchen, they looked in the empty study before going upstairs. Cyrus held Josephine's elbow for the ascent with a slightly caressing touch.

"The largest bedroom is across the front," Mathias said before turning for the back rooms.

The main bedroom boasted an antique woven rug, four-poster bed, and chaise lounge by the fireplace, not to mention side tables, dresser, and the dearest revolving bookcase two-shelves high.

"Isn't it lovely?" Josephine set the bookcase spinning, watching the empty shelves pass in a blur.

"Quaint, certainly." Cyrus studied her as she stroked the dark wood when it stopped.

"There's nothing sadder than an empty bookcase. It takes the soul right out of a house."

"You're enigmatic, Josephine Wolf, and I mean that with sincerest compliments."

She held his gaze several seconds before smiling. Cyrus was crisply handsome, almost beautiful. It felt unfair to the memory of her moments with Sean to enjoy the view and his words, so she dropped her gaze.

They finished their inspection of the two other bedrooms—both empty—and the generous bathroom before returning to the main floor.

"Now it's time for the basement apartment," Mathias said.

"I don't need to see your dungeon, brother. It can't be as enchanting as this space and this alone, being perfect for Cyrus, merits a thoughtful consideration."

"But it's large enough for the both of us. Perhaps you would want the dungeon for yourself. If Miss Jensen accepts Father's proposal, you could escape too."

"My herb sales don't make enough for me to live off of. Besides, there's no space for a garden like I have now."

"You could use pots on the balconies, and there's a bit of dirt along the sides of the house. Freedom!" When she didn't reply, Mathias shrugged. "Well, I've got to take a look at least. I told Mr. Melling we'd have the key back to his office by two."

"Mr. Melling?" The name had haunted Josephine since that Halloween night. That was what Sean had called the blond who'd voiced concern over her age when the leader was set on tormenting the girl.

"Alexander Melling. He's the lawyer for the wife in the Rupert Lyons divorce case. He's in jail on murder charges. The attack on the deceased woman happened here, though she died at the hospital. Mr. Lyons is in a heap of trouble for what he did. Surely you remember the reports from a month or two back."

Josephine shivered and nodded. She had known the moment she read about the events of Rupert Lyons beating a prostitute in some private love nest that they were true because a boy who would torment a five-year-old would be capable of any despicable act by the time he reached maturity.

"And that's not the oddest thing," Mathis continued. "The house was Alexander Melling's before Lyons bought it. Everything in here was chosen by or for Melling's fiancée in 1905 for a wedding that never happened. There are some wild rumors about what went on here then, but it was nothing that made it to court."

"Why would you want a house with this kind of history?" Josephine asked.

"Because it won't be shocked by whatever we do within these walls." Mathias sized her up a moment before continuing. "Your Mr. Spunner has connections to both those scandals, too. His name comes up as one of the guests at a debauched bachelor party here when Melling had the house, not to mention he was engaged to Melling's sister later that same year. Plus he was known to be friends to some degree with his fellow lawyer, Rupert."

"Lawyers are the worst," Cyrus stated. "They think they're above the law because they know all the judges."

Josephine wanted to say something to refute his claim but didn't know Sean well enough. After all, how much better was he than a typical cad by his actions with her that morning? What true gentleman would take a woman he's barely associated with into his home, have her feel him, and promise to discuss doing more?

But by incriminating Sean, Josephine would be saying poor things about herself. There was nothing she was ashamed of, even if she didn't want her brother and his friend knowing.

Seven

On her way home, Josephine saw Edgar Melvin scurry down the steps from the portico of the cathedral. Surprised at seeing him leave a place of worship without it being Sunday, she stopped at the front gate. Before reaching the sidewalk, he met Josephine's eye. Seeing it was her, he gave a curling sneer, but tipped his hat, flashing his red hair. When he passed in front of her, the scent of incense wafted by. He'd been in the cathedral long enough for the air to permeate his clothes.

Confused and anxious at seeing her old tormentor, Josephine took the Government streetcar west and checked behind her often. She sought solace in her bedroom as soon as she returned home. Being surrounded by the soft ruffles on the floral bedspread and curtains typically calmed her, but even after five minutes of petting Midnight, she was still agitated.

"Miss Cordelia is here for you!" Sarah called without finding out if Josephine was accepting visitors because she knew her best friend was always welcome.

Cordelia Barnes—heart-shaped face, dark hair, and garbed in all black—appeared to be in perpetual mourning or training for the convent. Considered an eccentric artist by most, Cordelia was often misunderstood but between them, they shared plenty of laughs with her wicked sense of humor.

"Hello, Del."

"Jo." She closed the door behind her and stopped in the middle of the room. "What happened to you?"

Josephine could never hide anything from her, so she didn't try. "I saw Edgar Melvin on my way home. It's been months since we've passed, but he still sneered at me."

Cordelia shook her head. "No, something more."

She smiled, thinking back earlier in the day. "I've been in a man's arms, had his tongue in my mouth, and felt his pulsing manhood beneath his trousers."

Her dark eyes widened. "How was it?"

"Glorious!" Josephine hugged Midnight before passing the cat to Cordelia. "I would have done more with him, but he insisted I think about it first. I have been thinking and there's no one else I'd rather be with for my first time."

"That's very chivalrous of him. Who's the lucky man to finally get a taste of you?"

"Sean Spunner."

"Older and most likely *very* experienced if he's anything like the men in his social circle."

"He confessed it's been a long time."

Cordelia laughed. "That could mean two weeks to a man like him."

"I don't think so. I haven't seen anyone at his house since his fiancée died."

"Eliza Melling. My brothers were crazy about her." Cordelia was the only girl in a family of five older brothers and envied Josephine's lone brother. "How often have you checked on Sean during your spirit ramblings?"

"Once a week or so. He's not always there, but when he is, he's alone in his library."

"Would you know if he had company in his bedroom?" Cordelia teased.

"I think I'd know, though he keeps those draped shut. I never go through walls at my friends' houses. That's rude."

"Astral manners, as if anyone would know if you broke them. But your Mr. Spunner has proven himself noble many times. When do you see him again?"

"Tomorrow. He said he wants to see my *garden*." Josephine giggled.

"And plant a few seeds there, I bet!"

They laughed so much, Josephine cried. Hugging Cordelia, she brought her onto the bed and turned serious. "I've loved him nearly my whole life, Del. If he refuses…I don't know what I'll do."

"You'll need French underwear and a low-cut dress for starters. My sisters-in-law swear by them."

"Thank you for supporting me."

"I can't support you better than a French corset." Cordelia laughed. "You're lucky, Jo. I'll probably decide to give up and turn for the cloisters when I reach twenty-five."

"But you might lose your perfect match. Just look at Miss Jensen and my father."

"No offense to your father, but I'd rather catch a man who isn't old enough to have grown children. I'd want a vigorous affair. How firm was Mr. Spunner when you touched him?"

"Aren't you wicked!"

"Well?" Her dark brows lifted.

"His arms are—"

"Not his arms, you ninny!"

Josephine laughed, her face heating. "It was virile. My whole body wanted to feel him—it was electric. I hope he arrives when he said he will."

"Has he ever let you down?"

She shook her head.

"Then have faith, Jo. Or prepare a love potion."

"You know I don't do things like that, Del."

"You could make a lot more money if you did."

***

At six forty-five that evening, Josephine sat in the parlor with her father. Mr. Wolf was in a tuxedo, nervously brushing his graying mustache with his left hand.

"You look handsome, Papa."

He crossed from his armchair to the sofa. "And you're a beautiful woman. When did you grow up, my little Josephine?"

"Sometime over these past years."

His hand gently traced her smile lines. "I'll always love your mother, and I thank you for shining this reminder of her on me so often. But you understand, don't you, Jo? I'm ready to share my life with someone once more."

She nodded.

"I wouldn't be surprised if you have your eye on a man yourself. I hope he's equal to the task." Mr. Wolf began pacing, nervously flipping the ring box in his pocket. "It's all different this time. Helen didn't get a ring until our wedding day, and that was only a plain band. These days it's all about the show of kneeling before a lady with a ring to dazzle her. I hope it's big enough for Marlene."

"If she truly loves you, the ring won't matter, though buying it from Willis and Percy is a great statement."

"I pray so." He sighed. "Where's Mathias?"

"Right here, Father. I shut Midnight in Jo's room so he doesn't jump on the dining table. Why do I have to wear a monkey suit when Jo looks like she always does?"

"I do not!" She looked down at her nicest ensemble. "Since when do I wear a Sunday dress to supper during the week?"

Papa frowned. "I should have thought of that. You need a few evening gowns, Jo. Maybe Marlene will go shopping with you if everything works out."

Caught between excitement and hurt, Josephine swallowed the sting that it took her father seeking marriage to be concerned about her attire. She was happy to be able to acquire some new dresses because a gown would be needed when the Mardi Gras invitation came.

When the knock sounded at precisely seven, Josephine went to the door as her father had requested. It was Marlene Jensen's first time in their home. Josephine had only spoken to her in passing at a few social gatherings since summer.

The brunette stood with perfect posture in a nauseating fox stole that hung from her shoulders above a green gown that accentuated her hourglass shape.

"Good evening, Miss Jensen. We are happy you could join us," Josephine said. "Please come in."

As the woman stepped inside, her parents' chauffeur drove away.

"May I take your wrap?"

"Thank you, Miss Wolf."

"Call me Jo or Josephine, please."

Trying not to grimace, Josephine placed the fur on the credenza so it wouldn't touch her own outerwear on the hall tree. Marlene was too busy checking her reflection in the mirror to notice the revulsion.

"Your hair looks lovely, Miss Jensen."

She turned and smiled, showcasing straight teeth. "And call me Marlene, Josephine, as your father does."

Josephine nodded and motioned toward the nearest doorway. "We're gathered in the parlor."

Mr. Wolf and Mathias both stood when they entered.

"Marlene," Mr. Wolf said as he approached with outstretched hands, "welcome to our humble home."

He kissed her cheek and she blushed.

"Thank you, Jesse. I'm pleased to be here."

"I believe you know my oldest, Mathias Neal."

Mathias offered his hand. "Thank you for coming, Miss Jensen."

"Please call me Marlene. I asked Josephine to do so as well."

Mr. Wolf took her elbow and sat beside her on the sofa rather than holding court in his preferred armchair. Seeing the spot by the hearth empty, Josephine took it for the first time in her life. Mathias smirked, but their father was too busy exchanging words with Marlene about the day's weather to notice.

He's nauseating, isn't he? Mathias asked.

I think it's sweet.

Don't tell me you've gone soft, Jo. Was it the attention from Mr. Spunner?

I'll never tell.

You don't have to. Your face says it all.

Seeing her father and Marlene engrossed in their own exchange, Josephine stood. "Mathias, will you come with me to check the dining room?"

Mr. Wolf cleared his throat as his children left. The last thing Josephine saw was his hand disappearing into his pocket.

Do you think she'll accept, Mat?

Fifty, fifty. She seems sincere, but it's a step down on the social ladder for her.

Papa's a fine catch, and if she brings some money along with her, she'll be able to sustain her lifestyle.

Not in this house.

Josephine's blood went cold. "But what of my garden?"

"Come with me so you don't have to worry about that. I'll put you in the dungeon until a prince comes to your rescue." Mathias said from across the table that glittered with silver.

"A princess should be in a tower, you ninny. You only ever care about things that affect yourself."

"Cyrus was smitten with you. He asked all sorts of questions after you left."

"I hope you told him all the horrible truths about me."

His grin accented the peak in his eyebrows—the angled arch above his brown eyes. "That you only change your underdrawers on Saturdays and you brew poisons with your herbs. Yes, all the important things."

She laughed but a shriek of joy from the front room was louder.

"I'll take that as a yes from Miss Jensen."

They waited a few minutes before returning to the parlor. Josephine's throat seized at seeing her father holding

Marlene, but her heart wanted to be happy for him. Now that she knew what it felt like to be held, Josephine wanted that experience for everyone.

"I assume congratulations are in order," Mathias said.

"Yes!" Mr. Wolf went to his feet, bringing Marlene with him.

Mathias hugged his father then kissed Marlene's cheek, and Josephine did the same.

"Thank you both for accepting me into your family," she said with all the sweetness one would expect from a glowing bride-to-be. "I look forward to getting to know y'all better in the coming months."

"When will the wedding take place?" Josephine asked.

"After Lent, but before it gets too hot," Marlene answered. "I think April would be perfect, don't you?"

"Certainly," Mr. Wolf said. "Now let me go see that we have a bottle of champagne to go with supper."

When they gathered in the dining room, Marlene was placed at the foot of the table. She seemed genuinely moved at being given that honor. Her eyes stayed misty, and she often studied the diamond adorning her left ring finger.

"I looked at a house for sale this afternoon, Father," Mathias announced over dessert.

Mr. Wolf paused while eating his slice of rum cake. "This is rather sudden."

"A friend I met last month has been in a hotel since he arrived in town. I've been helping him look for permanent residence and keeping an eye out for myself at the same time."

"You must be getting on well, Mathias," Marlene remarked.

"Very well, thank you. I've already advanced two levels in the accounting department since college graduation."

"Jesse has told me his children are clever." She looked at Josephine. "And he says you have a terrific green thumb. I'd love to see your garden when I come for Sunday dinner. I've heard stories about your herbal teas but have yet to try one."

"The garden isn't at its peak this time of year, but I'll happily show you."

"And we'll be sure to serve some of Jo's tea when you next visit," Mr. Wolf said.

After supper, Mr. Wolf took Marlene on a tour of the house while Mathias and Josephine took brandy in the parlor.

"He's old enough to be her father," Mathias remarked between sips of his drink.

"It's only fifteen years," Josephine said, thinking of the decade that separated her and Sean.

"Boys can father children at fifteen. They've done it for centuries." He smirked. "When I was of age, Papa told me a few stories from his youth that would curl your hair."

"I can't stand to think of our father doing anything sexual."

"He wouldn't be a father if he hadn't."

She rolled her eyes. "Still, it's nothing I want to visualize, thank you very much."

Mathias lit his cigarette as the sound of Marlene's laughter floated down the stairs. "I'll be glad I don't have to listen to them going at it when the time comes."

"You have months before the wedding, even if today's house doesn't come through. Maybe you'll find something closer."

"I'd like to be able to walk to restaurants and work without bothering with the streetcars. And your dungeon would await, sister."

"But how would it look if I'm courting a man and have my own apartment?"

He laughed. "What man wouldn't want to avoid parents and chaperones? Having easy access to you would be a blessing, not a hindrance."

"I don't want to be considered immoral by everyone. Have you ever…before?"

His toothy grin practically leered. "In more ways than you'll ever know."

Eight

After a night of impassioned dreams, Josephine rose early to work in the garden she had neglected the day before. With both Sean and Marlene inspecting the yard that weekend, it needed tending. Due to the cooler months, there were fewer weeds to deal with. She pruned the lavender, mint, and chives plus weeded around the green tea plants while Midnight dozed in the morning sun. Then Josephine inspected the shed where she did most of her herb drying. She checked the hanging herb bundles, wiped down the counter, and swept the floor.

By ten o'clock, both Mr. Wolf and Mathias were gone. Josephine went inside to wash so she'd be fresh when Sean arrived. Not wanting to look like she was trying too hard, she chose an old gingham dress best suited for summer chores and braided her hair in a single plait. A straw sunhat and gathering basket were her accessories.

While she was clipping a camellia blossom in the side yard, a hand went to her hip. Eyes wide, she turned to find Sean grinning at her.

He stepped back, looking crisp in a charcoal day suit and derby. "Good morning, Josephine. I hope it's all right I'm a few minutes early."

"Of course." She smiled in return though a shift in him she didn't understand unnerved her.

"Allow me to take your basket." He slipped the gathering basket from her forearm.

"This side of the yard isn't anything you haven't seen a dozen times around town, so let's move to the back."

He stayed at her elbow as they walked. "Is there good news about your family?"

"Marlene Jensen will be my father's wife this spring."

"She's an intelligent woman with a love for community work–your father is blessed to have found her. I'll be sure to have masquerade invitations delivered for everyone."

Sean was attentive and charming but also stilted as he followed her about. After showing him the medicinal and kitchen herb gardens, Josephine met his gaze across the rosemary.

"What happened at the party you attended last night?" she asked with trepidation.

"I met the most extraordinary woman." Sean's smile was bigger than ever, then he bit his lower lip making his chipped tooth all the more adorable.

"How exciting for you." Josephine tried not to let her disappointment show, but he wouldn't have noticed if it had.

"She's twenty-five, from Boston, and has the most cultured tone that she chided me with. She came to town to teach science to the girls at Barton Academy. You'd get along splendidly."

"I have no desire to meet her." She snatched the basket from his unsuspecting hand and marched to the shed.

Basket and hat on the counter, Josephine waited for him to seal her fate. Midnight jumped onto the ledge a moment before Sean entered.

"Jo, I didn't plan for what happened yesterday," he said.

"Between us or the woman you met?"

He cupped her cheek. "Both, darling."

"Did you kiss her?"

"We shared a few kisses and danced and talked."

Josephine shifted away from his touch. "When do you see her again?"

"I have no idea." He gave a nervous laugh. "I left that decision to her as a way to appease her feminist sensibilities."

"But you love her already."

"You're intuitive." He stepped closer, trapping her between his hard body and the counter, and tossed his hat next to hers. "I love this new connection with you, Jo, but I can't deny Hattie Fernsby stirred something in me last night."

"And that *something,* as you say, is more than what you feel for me. Is that because I'm still that scared five-year-old to you?"

"I thought we established that you're a woman, and my response to you is as nature intended."

When his hands grabbed her hips, she grasped his buttocks and held him firmly against her. "Damn you, Sean Spunner, for not allowing us to do more yesterday."

"I love your tenacity, Jo, but you know you'd be hurting even more than you think you are right now if we had enjoyed each other fully."

"But you might not have gone to the party or taken me with you instead!"

"No 'what ifs', darling. Any woman who grabs me by the ass isn't one to sit around moping. You'll be a feisty lover when the time comes, Jo."

"I'll give you until Christmas. If your science teacher doesn't get in touch with you—"

"You'll give me the sweetest present ever," he finished. "Thank you for understanding I need to give her a chance. But don't wait around for me. You're too wonderful for that, which I think Mr. Harrington would agree with. He seemed very keen on you when I stopped by the restaurant yesterday."

"I'm not sure I'd be comfortable stepping out with a friend of my brother's."

"You might not worry so much if you make a good connection."

"How could anything feel better than this?" She shifted against him.

"Jo, you're a natural minx." He devoured her mouth.

Who would have thought old Mr. Spunner would get fresh with my little sister?

Josephine gasped and turned to the open door.

"What a surprise, Mr. Spunner." Mathias smirked.

As calm as if he'd been seen discussing the weather, Sean slowly released Josephine from his arms and nodded at her brother. "Hello, Mathias. It's a beautiful day, isn't it?"

"Yes… it is." Mathias looked confused at the lack of stammering and excuses.

"Jo," Sean said as he took her elbow, "did that complete the garden tour or was there more to see outside?"

"That was it, but would you like some clippings to bring your cook?"

"Althea would enjoy that. Thank you." He handed Josephine her hat, then donned his own and took the gathering basket.

Mathias still stood in the doorway.

"Did you need something, Mat?" Josephine asked.

He gave a hearty guffaw and stepped to the side. "Not a thing." When they passed, he slapped Sean's shoulder. "Tread carefully, Mr. Spunner."

"I plan to. Your sister is a siren."

Josephine snipped parsley, dill, thyme, and more. Sean stayed at her side, watching the offerings fill the basket.

"Are you upset your brother found us?" he asked.

"I was at first, but not anymore."

"Don't be ashamed of your sexuality, Jo. It's a very real part of being human. When you start hiding from it, you lose yourself. You're the truest woman I've ever known. The world needs this bold Josephine Wolf."

"But do *you* need her?"

He fingered her cheek and ran his thumb along her bottom lip. "I want her."

Josephine gave a bittersweet smile, letting him know she'd rather him need her. Need was stronger, deeper, and had the potential to last longer than a passing fancy of want. He might want her now, but it could be because his new woman was untouchable for the time being. Would he want her tomorrow? Next week? Christmas?

"Would you like me to wrap the herbs for you?"

"That isn't necessary. I'll bring them home in the basket. You may collect it Monday evening, unless you'd rather I deliver it."

"I'll retrieve it."

"I look forward to your visit." He kissed her cheek and winked.

Midnight followed Josephine inside. The cat slipped quietly up the stairs, but Mathias pounced.

"Get in here and tell me what's going on with you and Mr. Spunner."

She rolled her eyes but sat across from him. "He's always been friendly, but after a few years of a dry spell, we struck up a reconnection yesterday morning."

"That's some connection in twenty-four hours, Jo. Was he always physical with you?" Mathias propped his foot on his opposite knee.

"I was nothing but a child all those other times we talked. Now that I'm in my twenties, that decade gap isn't so wide."

He dropped his foot to the floor and leaned forward from his seat. "Listen, I'm pledging to a society next month, but don't tell Father."

"Sean is going to invite us to Order of Mayhem's New Year's Eve ball."

"Those old men aren't the ranks I'll be joining. Mardi Gras is another reason I want to move out. I'll be coming and going a lot and don't want to have to answer questions from Father or Sarah."

"I know better than to ask which society it is."

Good, because I don't want to say Mystics of Dardenne aloud. Miss Sarah might wash my mouth out with soap.

Josephine laughed. *You would join the most notorious krewe. They don't even parade and that's the best part about Mardi Gras.*

You can't say that until you've attended a masquerade. Besides, they would parade if the city let them, but Dardennes don't have the best track record with law enforcement.

Yet you want to join them despite that.

I want to join them because of that. Mathias grinned and stood. Tweaking his sister's nose as he passed, he said aloud, "No matter what, Jo, I'll be here for you."

✳✳✳

On Sunday morning, Mr. Wolf attended late Mass with Marlene at the cathedral. Josephine and Mathias were under instructions from their father to be in the parlor when they returned to dine together for Sunday dinner, though nothing afterward would be forced.

"I don't know what to think about him going to Mass when it isn't a holiday. I'm glad he isn't asking us to attend with him." Mathias exhaled a tight smoke ring. "Nor has he forbidden smoking in the parlor. When I get my own place, I'll smoke at the dinner table."

"What will your future wife say?"

"There won't be one of those if I have anything to say about it."

Circling a finger over the scrolling arm of the chair, Josephine smirked. "I suppose you find all the companionship you need without those strings."

"Damn right I do, Jo. Marriages are a sham most of the time. What our parents had was a miracle these days. Most men would have spent their downtime at a club or whorehouse rather than sitting beside their wife's bed for two years, watching her die." He took a deep drag. "Seeing how a husband should be is one of the many ways I'll never measure up to our father."

"That's rather dismal, even for you."

Mathias waved his cigarette toward the room. "This house is trapped in the previous century. Not a whit of it has been redecorated from how Mama set things when we were kids. Even if Moneybags Marlene agrees to stay here, she'll gut the place of every ruffle. That's more than love that would allow Papa to sit by and watch that happen. That's a level of patience and self-mastery I don't have."

"You'll find someone to put up with you, brother."

He flashed his debonair grin. "I need someone who will worship me, dear sister."

"Del thinks you're the handsomest man in Mobile."

"Cordelia Barnes is even odder than you, and that's saying a lot, though she does appear to have fine taste in men." He crushed the butt of his cigarette into the crystal ashtray on the coffee table. "Funny, I always assumed she'd be in a convent by now."

"She's waiting a few more years. If she's still single, she plans to join so she won't be a blight on her family."

"And you, Jo?" He looked me over. "Getting physical with an established lawyer is risky. Do you plan on trapping him into marriage?"

"I'll never force a man to marry me."

"Then I hope you're careful or know what to do should things get away from you. I suppose you have the means in the garden."

"Whatever are you talking about?"

"The true witch of Mobile, Old Lady Rettig."

A heaviness passed through Josephine's chest at the memory of the afternoons and summers she spent with the woman. "She wasn't a witch."

Mathias laughed. "Why do you think your nickname held so long? By the time it was slipping from people's memory you had to go and befriend that woman."

"So?"

"All the older boys and girls knew she was the medicine women society strumpets visited when they went too far. She fixed them a nice herbal cocktail to make their problems go away. I'm surprised someone hasn't turned up here asking you for one."

Josephine's mouth gaped as she stared at him over the forbidden topic.

He shook his head. "You were naïve, but I'd have thought you would have figured that out by now. The only thing more promiscuous than a drunk debutante is a buck rabbit in spring."

Before Josephine could remark on the knowledge she'd acquired from Mrs. Rettig's books, their father's automobile pulled to a stop on the side of the house. Josephine moved to the far armchair, leaving both her father's seat and the sofa open. Mathias waited at the front door to welcome them.

"Allow me to take your coats," he said once they entered.

"It was a lovely service," Marlene said as she swept into the parlor. "Advent is special every year. I do wish y'all would go with us next Sunday."

"I'll be at the Christmas Eve service," Josephine told her.

"But—"

"Jo and Mat are old enough to make their own decisions," Mr. Wolf said, then left a kiss on her cheek as they sat together on the sofa.

"Just call us heathens," Mathias said with a devilish smile.

Marlene wrinkled her nose.

"Mass or not," Mr. Wolf said, "I've always loved Sunday dinners with the family."

There was an awkward silence, followed by a knock at the door. Josephine excused herself, grateful to escape even if only for a moment.

Andrew Graves, Merritt's son, stood blushing on the porch in the full uniform of a Mardi Gras court page. The white and gold costume matched the pillow he extended, on which sat four envelopes.

"Thank you."

As soon as Josephine took them, he ran through the park, tossing the pillow and catching it as he went to his home on the Chatham Street side—no doubt to hastily remove the tights and silk Sean had wrangled him into.

The envelopes were marked for Jesse, Mathias, Marlene, and Josephine.

"We had a delivery by Mardi Gras page," she announced, handing each person their envelope.

As expected, it was an invitation to the Order of Mayhem's New Year's Eve ball. Tucked inside Josephine's was a small note that read "No matter what, save a dance for me." Smiling, she looked at the others.

"I had no idea you were acquainted with members of the society," Marlene said to Mr. Wolf. "I typically attend with my parents, but it will be lovely to go with you."

"Jo, now you really need to go shopping." Papa looked at his fiancée. "Josephine doesn't have a gown, and her Sunday finery could use a boost."

Josephine ran a hand over her blue skirt, realizing that she'd had it for a couple years.

"I could pick you up tomorrow, Josephine, and bring you to Mademoiselle Bisset's," Marlene said. "She's the only one to trust for special occasions. One word to her, and she'll send the bill to your father's office with an immediate credit for anything you want."

"That's sounds fine, Jo," her father said. "Get yourself two gowns and the same for Sundays."

"And whatever extras are needed," Marlene added with a squeeze to his arm. "Women often need new foundation pieces and accessories to complete an ensemble."

"Of course," he agreed. "It's well overdue, at any rate. Will you take Marlene up on her offer to assist you?"

Never having felt so shabby, Josephine nodded. "Yes, thank you. It's very generous of you to give up your time."

"I consider it an investment in the future, Josephine. How does ten o'clock sound?"

"Perfect." She forced a smile and refused to look at Mathias's mocking face.

Nine

As soon as Josephine climbed into the back of the Jensens' automobile Monday morning, she realized she had made a mistake. Marlene looked her over, not with contempt, but with enough of a criticizing eye to be slightly offensive.

"Is that the best you have for daytime?" Marlene fingered the navy skirt. "The quality is good, but it's plain. That shirt might as well be a man's as it has no flare."

Keeping herself in check so she wouldn't disgrace her father, Josephine counted to five before replying. "It's served me well, Marlene."

"Not too well. Jesse says you've never had a beau."

"I don't base my productivity in life on how often men flirt with me."

She smiled. "That's very sensible, Josephine, but your father worries about you. He wants me to be sure you get something dazzling. He fears he's been too lax with you in regard to bringing you up as a proper young lady."

Josephine turned to the window rather than look at Marlene. Her tone wasn't malicious, but it still stung. Marlene didn't understand Josephine's love for gardening and herbs, and she had no inkling of sharing any of her other interests with her future stepmother. Marlene would probably think telepathy and astral projection were devilry.

Mademoiselle Bisset's store was nestled in the heart of the shopping district. Thinking of Cordelia's words about French underwear helped excitement outweigh any misgivings.

If Josephine could somehow acquire provocative undergarments without Marlene seeing, she would be confident about her forthcoming attempt at seduction.

"It's good to see you, Miss Jensen," a brunette woman in a classic black dress said as soon as they entered, "though I thought you were already well-attired for the season."

"I am, thanks to you, Mademoiselle. Today I'm here in support of my fiancé's daughter, Josephine Wolf."

Her eyes widened, then she took Marlene's left hand to her bosom—after discreetly checking out the ring. "Congratulations, Miss Jensen!" Releasing the hand, the shopkeeper turned to Josephine. "Miss Wolf, I am sorry to say I am not acquainted with your family, but I have heard of your herbal skills from those who enjoy your teas. I received a few pouches as a gift last year and enjoyed the spicy flavor of the blend. I welcome you to my store and congratulate you on winning such a dear addition to your household."

"Thank you." Josephine smiled at the warm welcome, wishing she could deal with the owner without Marlene.

"Now my dear, turn around." Mademoiselle Bisset examined every inch of her for a good while. "Your complexion and bone structure are wonderful, your shape fine, though I think it is hiding under these plain clothes. Are you a woman of leisure?"

"I work almost daily in my garden."

"Ah! You must not be afraid to have clothes for the garden and clothes for the rest of the time, Miss Wolf. It is not indulgent to wear more than one outfit a day, especially if they are hung properly in between, allowing you to get more than one wear out of them."

"She's had no mother to guide her for almost two decades," Marlene remarked.

Mademoiselle Bisset tilted her head as she gazed at Josephine. "But you have done well for yourself, Miss Wolf, despite your loss. Now, for what occasion are you here?"

"Evening gowns," Josephine said before Marlene could take over, "and Sunday outfits. My father wishes me to have two of each."

"Yes, and you're to send the bill to Jesse Wolf," Marlene added. "He's a statistics man at the largest shipping firm on the river."

"How industrious. It is no wonder Miss Wolf likes to keep busy with her hands. What colors do you prefer, my dear?"

"Greens," Josephine replied.

Mademoiselle Bisset smiled and nodded. "Not jewel toned, but an earthy palette to match your garden."

"Won't that be too plain?" Marlene questioned.

Her lips went into a playful pout. "Do you not trust me by now, Miss Jensen? Go to the glove counter, and Collette will show you the latest arrivals. You need something new to go with that splendid diamond."

After Marlene was redirected, the owner led Josephine to the curtained dressing area.

"Thank you," she whispered as Mademoiselle closed them inside the pink-striped room.

"My dear, it must be overwhelming for you to come here with a woman who wishes to be a mother-figure when you are accustomed to being your own woman. I will do my best to make this an enjoyable experience."

"You're wonderful." Josephine sighed. "I wish I had known to come here on my own."

She patted Josephine's hand. "Now, Miss Wolf, my policy is to have every lady's measurements done so we can supply the proper foundation pieces. And an attendant must always be with you when trying on dresses. It is to protect my gowns and make sure the changing happens with ease. Do you have a lady's maid or have you ever been assisted before?"

"No, I'm afraid not, Mademoiselle."

"I will see to you myself this time, Miss Wolf. Do not be afraid to ask questions or tell me if you are uncomfortable."

Josephine nodded and disrobed. Mademoiselle didn't speak until Josephine was down to her under layers before the claw-foot mirror.

"It is good you are not too shy. Some on their first trip are a shade of blush by this point. Your skin is marvelous. No matter what the fashion magazines say, men adore a dusting of freckles."

Mademoiselle Bisset produced a measuring tape and small notebook from her pocket. After she recorded the numbers, Josephine caught her eye.

"I'd like something…" She put her hands under her breasts and lifted them through the chemise, creating cleavage where there wasn't much before.

Mademoiselle Bisset nodded.

"And pieces meant to be seen, but please don't show them to Miss Jensen," Josephine whispered.

Mademoiselle Bisset winked, then called out to one of her shop girls. She handed the paper with Josephine's measurements to the worker through a small parting of the curtain and gave her instructions in rapid French to bring an assortment of undergarments in the proper sizes.

When Mademoiselle turned back, she smiled. "You have natural poise, Miss Wolf. And your self-assurance is refreshing. Most women do not request what they truly want on their first visit—if ever. I appreciate your honesty."

"Oh, Mademoiselle, if only my father had met you!" Josephine breathed with awe over her graciousness.

She laughed. "My dear, by the end of the day I am cantankerous. I would not be pleasant to come home to after helping customers all day."

They were laughing when a box with the same striped pattern as the curtains was passed in.

"Give us five minutes," Mademoiselle told the worker. "Now, Miss Wolf, see what you like."

The lid of the box was lifted, revealing a myriad of lace and silk undersets and shapewear.

Josephine caught her breath. "I had no idea they could be so beautiful."

"Which will you try first?"

Josephine hastily removed her pathetic cotton set and went for the black ruffled drawers, topping it with a fitted silk camisole. She looked down at her breasts, which weren't all too different than before.

"To get what you want, we must add the corset." Mademoiselle wrapped a rigid contraption around her middle. It firmly set Josephine's posture and pushed up her breasts.

Feeling the increased mounds, Josephine smiled. "Yes, this is wonderful."

"Wait until you see it with a gown."

"Mademoiselle?" a voice called from the other side.

"You are just in time." She reached through the opening and produced an elegant plum gown of velvet and silk.

Josephine was speechless as Mademoiselle guided it over her head. When she looked in the full-length mirror, her hands immediately went to the creamy expanse of skin displayed between her throat and bosom above the squared neckline.

"Has that ever been displayed before?" Mademoiselle Bisset asked.

"No." Josephine laughed. "It's my first evening gown."

"You are lovely, my dear. The next gown I have for you is lighter. It could be used into spring, unlike this winter one."

The second gown required Josephine to change undersets, but she loved the new foundation pieces and the tiered sage and gold gown.

"When will I get to see a dress on her?" Marlene called.

"At the masquerade, along with everyone else!" Mademoiselle answered cheerily. "A woman likes to keep a few secrets in life."

Josephine spontaneously hugged the shopkeeper. "You understand everything, don't you?"

"I live to see joy on the faces of all who walk through my doors," she replied.

Then it was time for the Sunday finery, which could be used whenever Josephine needed something out of the ordinary. She settled on an orange two-piece walking suit that reminded her of the color of a sunset, and a robin's egg blue ensemble. Both accented her figure, complimented her coloring, and were tastefully stylish without being fussy.

Josephine opted to wear the orange set with the A-line skirt out of the store, along with a new pair of boots, a silky white underset, and gloves. The other new pieces and her old clothing would be delivered to the house that afternoon. Mademoiselle Bisset assured her the receipt for her father would not include itemized information about the undergarments, to which Josephine thanked her.

"Now," Marlene said as they climbed into the back of her automobile, "we're on to Klosky's to meet my mother for dinner."

"But I'm not prepared for that."

"Of course you are, Josephine. You look better than ever in your new clothes, and Mother has been dying to meet Jesse's children. I'm not the only one who wishes you and Mathias attended Mass."

As soon as they arrived at the restaurant, Josephine was subjected to scrutiny at the hands of Mrs. Jensen.

"You're such a pretty thing, Miss Wolf. It's a wonder you aren't spoken for already. Don't you think her coloring favors her father, Marlene?"

"Very much."

"At least she's kept a pale complexion when she works so much outdoors."

The Jensens chatter continued, and Josephine's eyes roamed to the high ceiling, wishing she could fly to the decorative glass above.

When their orders were placed, scorn over her meatless meal came to the forefront.

"You cannot eat like a bird, Josephine," Mrs. Jensen said. "Men like to see a woman indulge in a few of the finer things in life."

"She didn't eat the lovely roast the cook prepared yesterday," Marlene complained to her mother.

"We typically have fish on Sundays, but Papa wanted something more traditional with your visit because we'd just had fish on Friday," Josephine explained.

"Fish on Fridays is one thing, but multiple times a week is repugnant," Mrs. Jensen said with a lift of her sharp chin.

After the waiter delivered their food and stepped away, another man came to Josephine's side.

"I thought that was you, Miss Jo." Cyrus's suave good looks were on full display in his blue three-piece suit.

"Hello, Cyrus." Josephine offered her hand, and he kissed the back of it. "Let me introduce my father's fiancée, Miss

Jensen, and her mother, Mrs. Jensen. Ladies, this is Cyrus Harrington, a friend of Mathias."

"My heartfelt congratulations, Miss Jensen, and Mrs. Jensen. It's a pleasure to meet you both. I won't intrude any longer because I need to get back to my business luncheon, but I wanted to pay my respects to Jo." He took her hand once more for a parting kiss. "I hope to see you soon."

When Cyrus walked away, Mrs. Jensen turned to her daughter. "Did you look at him? He's the handsomest man I've seen in years! Miss Wolf, I hope you understand what an honor it is to be singled out like that."

Josephine shrugged and gave a dismissive smile. "He's polite, Mrs. Jensen."

"Men paying respects to be polite do not engage in unnecessary physical contact."

Marlene giggled. "Should I inform your father, Josephine?"

She spent the remainder of the meal fielding questions about Cyrus.

What seemed like eons later, they stood to leave.

Cyrus returned to the table at the same moment. "My meeting is now complete. May I escort you to your next appointment, ladies?"

"We're going to our automobile to bring Josephine home, but you're welcome to walk us out," Marlene told him as she hooked her arm around his. "Josephine told us you've done interior design. Do you specialize in residential or business?"

"I do both, but homes are my favorite, Miss Jensen."

"Do you have room on your schedule this winter or will you be too busy with the Mardi Gras tableaus? The Wolfs' house is positively last century. I'd love to have it freshened before the wedding this spring."

Cyrus glanced at Josephine's slight frown before focusing back on Marlene. "I'd be happy to see what I could do."

"Splendid." She artfully retrieved her calling card from the reticule at her wrist. "Let me know when we can meet, Mr. Harrington. Here's our car."

Seeing their approach, the chauffeur opened the back door. Cyrus handed in Miss Jensen, then her mother. He paused to look Josephine over after he took her hand.

"You're a vision, Jo. I'm glad I came across you."

"I'm sure," she said with a naughty smile, "because it appears to have scored you a big commission."

He laughed and decorously kissed her cheek. "Stay impudent, Jo."

Ten

"Marlene was right in bringing me to Mademoiselle Bisset," Josephine told her father over supper while stroking Midnight, who was in her lap. "She knows how best to sincerely flatter her customers. I hope I didn't spend too much."

"It's worth it to give you this experience you should have had years ago. Consider it an early birthday gift. Do you forgive my neglect?"

"Papa, I've never been neglected. I hope Marlene doesn't make you feel that way. I've loved my life with you and Mat." She looked into his hazel eyes. "I've wanted for nothing. What more could a girl need than a garden and a cat?"

Mr. Wolf and Mathias both laughed.

"Cyrus was as impressed as ever with you today," Mathias said. "He stopped by my office this afternoon and raved about you, Jo. He's pleased we received invitations to the Order of Mayhem ball so we can witness his Mardi Gras tableau design."

"Who is Cyrus?" Mr. Wolf asked.

"Cyrus Harrington is a designer from Atlanta. His father owns an architecture firm there, but he wanted to break away and do his own thing. He's here in town to work design jobs—tableaus, floats, florals, and interiors. I met him last month and we had dinner with Jo on Friday. He can't stop talking about her, especially after seeing her at Klosky's with the Jensens."

"Jo is exceptionally pretty today."

Josephine smiled, hoping Sean would think she was beautiful as well. "Just so you know, Father, Marlene has plans to hire Cyrus to redo the house, and it sounds like she wants it done before the wedding."

"She asked me about changing some of the furniture and wall colors when I showed her around this weekend. I'm glad she found someone to see to it."

"Cyrus is pricey," Mathias warned. "I hope you can afford it."

"She's using her own money and said it would be her wedding gift to the family. I welcomed her to do what she likes everywhere except in your and Jo's rooms, and the kitchen unless she gets Sarah's input. I hope you'll both support Marlene in this endeavor."

"Yes, Father, though I won't be around much longer." Mathias held the stare that came his way before explaining. "Cyrus put in an offer on a building with two units. If his offer is accepted, I plan to rent the smaller apartment from him."

He gave a knowing nod. "I hate to lose you, son, but I wish you well if this works out. I'm surprised you haven't left before now."

"I didn't want to leave you with only Jo for company. Now that Marlene is coming, it will be fine for both of you. But who knows. Maybe Jo will catch the eye of someone at the masquerade."

At the end of the meal, Mr. Wolf looked at Mathias. "Why don't we have a drink?"

Nudging Midnight off her lap, Josephine quietly excused herself so she could go to Sean's house as planned. Careful to make sure Midnight didn't follow her, she hastily pulled the front door closed.

Josephine walked the southern edge of Washington Square and down Augusta Street, headed for Rapier Avenue in the mild December night. The soft glow through the closed draperies was as welcoming as the porch lights. She climbed the steps and knocked.

A woman darker than the sky opened the door.

"May I help you?" Her knowing eyes looked Josephine over as she waited for a reply.

"I'm Jo Wolf. Sean told me I could collect my basket this evening."

Her gaze narrowed at the same time Sean emerged from his library, jacketless and with his shirtsleeves rolled to his elbows.

"That's Jo, who gave me all those herbs you raved about. Don't make her stand there, Althea." She moved aside and Sean took Josephine's hand, bringing her into the hall. "Don't you remember? She's the one the boys used to pick on, but now she would bring them to their knees."

Althea gave him a sharp look. "I know who she is. I'll get the basket."

Before either could speak, Althea returned.

"Don't rush her off," Sean said as he took the basket from his housekeeper.

"I was about to go home," she replied.

"Go on then. We'll be fine."

"Do you need coffee or anything?"

"Althea, I know how to attend to things, but thank you. I'll see you tomorrow."

Once the woman turned for the back hall with a matronly sigh, Sean set the basket on the credenza and led Josephine into the parlor. Stopping under the chandelier, he looked over every inch of her while biting his lower lip and rubbing a few days' growth of hair on his jaw.

"I'd know Mademoiselle Bisset's handiwork anywhere." He trailed a finger down the line of pearl buttons on the front of Josephine's top. "She's wonderful, isn't she?"

"Yes, and I found the loveliest gown for the masquerade. It's—"

"Did you know orange is my favorite color? It's seldom worn by ladies these days, but I adore everything about it. Cheerful, fiery, and bold." His hands trailed her sleeves, then around her shoulders. "It looks perfect on you, Jo."

Emboldened by the desire in his eyes and the Parisian lingerie beneath her ensemble, Josephine turned playful. "The jacket is a little warm. I'd like to remove it."

Grinning, Sean watched her undo the buttons. When the jacket was halfway opened, he settled in an armchair—legs sprawled, eyes hungry.

Jacket off, Josephine gently draped it over a side chair. She recalled her spirit wanderings through the red-light district the time Francesca and Cordelia had questions about sex when they were sixteen. Josephine had reported back more anecdotes than they could handle without giggling and blushing. Now Josephine used that knowledge as she returned to center stage in Sean's parlor.

"The blouse is pretty, isn't it?" She opened the top two buttons of the cream-colored shirt, then ran her hands over it. "It's so thin it's practically invisible. Can you see my new undergarments through it?"

"You don't play fair, Jo. You were supposed to wait for Christmas to advance things." He offered his hand and guided her to sit on his left knee.

"We agreed on Christmas for the full act, but there is much we could explore while we wait for consummation."

"Hellfire and brimstone, Jo! How could no man have discovered you before now?"

"None of them wanted a witch." She kissed his lips, avoiding his scruffy jaw, then below his ear as he'd done to her Friday.

He groaned and his hands fumbled over the blouse. Working the remaining buttons opened as they kissed, she did the same to him with less effective results. Sean's shirt was still tucked into his pants when he dropped hers to the floor.

Grabbing her hips, he shifted Josephine as he stood. "Wrap your legs around me and hold on."

Boots crossed at the ankles and arms around his shoulders, a thrill ran through her body as he mounted the stairs. He set her on a large bed with a purple coverlet and dropped to his knees to remove her boots. His own shoes and shirt were off when he joined her on the bed.

Golden brown eyes locked on her, his deep voice rumbled with want. "Are we still in agreement?"

"Yes, Sean. I want to know passion and pleasure."

His face went to the display at her chest, kissing the mounds that bulged above the edge of the white chemise thanks to the corset. The attentions started gently, but he was soon tonguing the cleavage. Not knowing what to do, Josephine wiggled and arched while trying to hold still as his abrasive chin stubble inflamed her skin.

"Don't fight it, Jo. Feel everything." Sean laid back, bringing her on top of him. He kept his face buried in her chest, but his hands worked open the corset stays. "There, darling. Breathe."

The shapewear fell to the floor, and he positioned her to straddle him at the groin, the orange skirt billowing around them. His hands were on her back, but his eyes roamed from her chest to her face. His hips began a slight movement, barely perceptible to her in her inflamed state, but the primitive rhythm was one Josephine instinctively knew. She answered with a grinding motion that stoked the fire.

"Yes, darling. That's it."

His hands felt every inch of her breasts through the thin undergarment. She sighed and held back a moan.

"Get those beauties up here, Jo." He bucked against her from below, pushing her up his torso with each movement until her chest was in line with his face.

With a wicked smile, his right hand pulled down the chemise as his mouth met skin. Josephine shuddered as his hands and tongue worked in tandem, coaxing her into riots of ecstasy. He pulled the skirt higher until he could reach underneath, then skimmed her stockings above the knees and followed the garter straps that were attached to the bottom of the ruffled underdrawers, deftly undoing them. He caressed and teased. Then his hands went under that final layer, gripping her hips.

"Ride me hard, Jo. Get what you need."

Sean slid her down to his groin, pressed their connection firmer with a steady tempo from below, and assisted her movements by manipulating her hip motions. How he managed to keep doing it all was baffling, but Josephine couldn't concentrate on his display of strength and coordination while racing to the edge of something magical.

"Sean!"

"I'm here for you, darling."

She locked eyes with him as her body tensed until fireworks blinded her. She collapsed on his chest, her spirit drifting toward the ceiling. She vaguely noticed his hug and kisses when she returned to her body.

"Climax looks wonderful on you." His kiss was soft and deep as he rolled them onto their sides, bringing Josephine out of languidness.

"That was incredible! When can we do it again?"

"It's a heady rush—completely addicting—but that needs to be it for tonight." Sean kissed her cheek and sat up chuckling. "I spent in my pants. Lord, I haven't played like this since I was school-aged, but I needed that release. Thank you, darling. Give me a minute to get something clean, then I'll help you find your clothes."

Sean disrobed on his way out, lastly dropping his underdrawers in the hall. Josephine watched his tight backside until he disappeared through the open door across the hall. Wondering why he didn't change in that room, she sat up to observe the space as she secured her stockings. It was bare of any personal items beside what they'd strewn about.

He'd brought her to a spare bedroom!

Indignant, Josephine marched across the hall, not bothering to cover the friction burns on her chest. Sean was pulling on a pair of brown trousers in front of his open closet.

"How dare you, Sean Spunner!"

Eyes wide, he turned with an innocent twist to his sensual mouth.

"You brought me to a guestroom! Am I not good enough for your own bed?"

He caressed her shoulder. "Darling, it's nothing shameful."

She knocked his hand away. "Don't *darling* me. I have a name, you know."

"Yes, Josephine Wolf," Sean chided, "I'm aware of your name and you have nothing to be upset over. Althea keeps all the rooms spotless. You're good enough for any bed in my house, but I didn't want your scent on my pillows. That would make it difficult for me to sleep."

"Because you can't be bothered to think of me when I'm gone? Or is it because you hope to bring that teacher here and can't have the scent of another woman on your sheets? You're a selfish louse. I'll not be used like this, Sean!"

He had the audacity to laugh. "Who was it that came to me to ask me to show her passion? It sounds like you wanted to use me first, Jo."

Trembling with anger, Josephine crossed her arms. "So you admit to using me! And don't forget you had no objection to my request, waiting all of two seconds before sticking your tongue down my throat."

"But you came here tonight, once again." He attempted to disarm her with a charming smile.

"Because you stole my basket!"

"I don't want your basket." Sean's voice was so low he practically growled.

"No, you want these!" She cupped her breasts, lifting them to him like an offering. "And my sex, but only if your chosen one doesn't respond to you in the next few weeks. Guess what? I hope that teacher does. Then I can tell her how you amused yourself with me while you waited for her!"

"You practically begged me to explore with you. You wanted my expertise and played the siren to get it. Don't be sore when you discover you're not in control like you thought you were."

With tears smarting her eyes, she turned away. "Even your housekeeper tried to spare me this indignity. You're old enough to know better, Sean."

"So are you, Jo, even if you lack the experience." His hand went to her shoulder. "Most women your age are married with children, unless they're career girls. But even then, they've had a liaison or two."

She turned on him, eyes blazing. "What do you think this has all been about? I want those things but have been denied them because stupid Edgar Melvin branded me a witch that Halloween!"

Tear-blinded, she tripped on Sean's pants and then her corset before stumbling onto the purple bed in defeat.

Jo? Are you all right? Where are you?

Startled, her smattering of tears stopped. *You have impeccable timing, Mat.*

You're not in your room. Don't tell me you left the house to meet Mr. Spunner.

She wiped her eyes. *Then I won't tell you.*

It's nearly ten. When are you coming home?

As soon as I get my corset and—

Don't tell me you had sex with that bounder!

I might have made a few miscalculations, but that's not one of them. I'll be home before long.

Josephine sat up, blinking to clear the final tears that clung to her lashes as she tied her boots.

"Where did you go?" Sean asked from the door.

"I'll be gone as soon as possible. Excuse me for sullying your space."

"No." He crossed the room and took her arm. "You were right there, but it was like your mind was gone. There was this intensity—I could feel something in the air."

She shook her head. "I just want to get dressed and leave."

His large hands flexed around her arm as he leaned closer.

I said to leave me alone, you bastard!

Sean jerked away, staring. "What did you do?"

Josephine inwardly groaned at forgetting anyone might be able to hear. It was too late to hide, so she figured she might as well enjoy it.

Nothing more than a witch ought to do when an arrogant man makes a nuisance of himself. Hand me my corset before I turn you into a toad.

"Why didn't you tell me you're telepathic, Jo?"

He was too well-read to not understand what she did. Josephine walked around him, snatched the corset off the floor and held it up so she could see which way it went. "Would that have made a difference?"

"Yes!" His eyes gleamed with a lust for something other than flesh. "What else can you do?"

"I'm not a circus monkey." She attempted the fasteners on the corset three times unsuccessfully in her agitated state. "Make yourself useful, or I'll walk out of the house with my underclothes on one shoulder and your soiled drawers on the other."

He laughed and pulled the corset into place. Once it was fastened, he turned her to face him. "I've made a study of phenomena like this before—mediumship, invocators, spiritualism—but have never known a telepath. You should have told me."

"I'm either good enough for you or I'm not. You already made it clear I'm not your first choice."

"But that was before I knew."

"Do you hear yourself? You were dismissing everything about me moments ago but now you're begging for my affection because of something I can do. I hope that release lasts until your teacher arrives because I'm done with you, Sean. My childhood infatuation is officially over."

Josephine hurried to the parlor, retrieved her blouse from the floor, and slipped it on. Sean stopped in the doorway while she buttoned the jacket. Giving him as wide a berth as possible wasn't enough to get to the hall unscathed.

His hand went to her forearm. "I do care for you, Jo."

"Obviously not as much as you care for yourself." She shook off his touch and grabbed her basket. "I hope you sleep well on your scentless pillow."

When she reached the edge of Washington Square, Mathias was waiting for her.

Let's go home, Jo. Things will look better in the morning.

She nodded, grateful for her brother's understanding.

Eleven

On Wednesday, Josephine played hostess to Marlene and Cyrus for a business luncheon to discuss changes within the Wolf house. Cyrus was ready with smiles for Josephine whenever he wasn't taking notes, though Marlene's watchful eyes were forever on them.

"I have cousins who come to town," Marlene said in the spare bedroom on their post-dinner tour, "and I'd like to be able to host rather than them always staying with my parents. Between this room and Mathias's, it will be plenty. I want the main bedroom done last. Jesse will move to one of the guest rooms when it's worked on and stay there until the wedding so we both have a fresh start with it when I move in."

While Marlene energetically poked around Mr. Wolf's bedroom, Cyrus stood nonchalantly beside Josephine and tilted his notepad in her direction.

Would you have supper with me Friday?

The words were bold in the middle of the page and Josephine had to hide her smile when Marlene looked over.

"Do you think this is the best location for the bed, Mr. Harrington?"

His eyes swept the room twice. "It's the only option for a double or larger, Miss Jensen. The placement of the doorways leaves no possible alternative, but with the new trimmings it will feel like a fresh space."

"My mother didn't die here, Marlene, if you're worried about that." Josephine's voice was uncharacteristically soft. "She was too weak for the stairs her final year, so Papa made over his study to fit a single bed for her. He often slept in the chair beside her."

"Oh, how thoughtful of him." Marlene looked away. "Let me inspect the tile in the bathroom."

She disappeared into the adjacent bath, and Cyrus raised his eyebrows at Josephine.

"Well, Jo, will you?"

"Supper Friday sounds lovely, Cyrus. Thank you. Will it be formal?"

"Casual, if that's all right with you."

"Perfectly." Josephine smiled over the plans for her first official outing with a man, not counting her disastrous evening with Sean.

"I'll arrive for you at seven-thirty. Thank you for the honor of dining with you." Cyrus's free hand briefly clasped hers.

"The tiles are in great condition," Marlene called. "I believe blues would go well in here for the trimmings. I don't care for this red at all. Come see, Mr. Harrington."

Midnight prowled the corners of the bedroom that was often closed to him. When the cat jumped onto Mr. Wolf's bed, Josephine picked him up before Marlene came out of the bathroom, Cyrus following.

"And Josephine's room," Marlene said, looking at her.

"That's hardly necessary after everything else," she said.

"Nonsense. I'm sure you'd like a bit of sprucing in there. Go with her, Mr. Harrington. I'll wait in the kitchen. There are things to discuss with Sarah before I can move forward in that space." Marlene winked at Josephine when she went for the door.

Cyrus followed Josephine into her room. She set Midnight on the bed, and he curled onto one of the pillows. When she turned from the cat, Cyrus grinned.

"You don't plan on being here long, do you?"

"I'm not jumping ship as quickly as Mat, but I'm keeping my options open." She shyly looked away, cheeks rosy.

"Tell me what you prefer, and I'll incorporate Miss Jensen's likes into it so she doesn't feel the need to change things when you move out."

"Medium-toned woods, nothing too ornate but beyond the square functionality of Craftsman. I enjoy a sensual curve on a well-turned piece of furniture."

"Go on." Cyrus closed the distance between them, brushing against her side.

"It's true," she whispered.

"I don't doubt you, Jo." His fingers trailed her hand before he left with a dashing grin.

At supper that night, Mathias was out, so it was only Mr. Wolf and Josephine at the table.

"Marlene's visit wasn't too hard on you, was it, Sarah?" Mr. Wolf asked when she carried in the platter of red fish.

"Of course not, Mr. Wolf. She has some lovely ideas to brighten the place. And Mr. Harrington is a gracious man."

"Everyone knows Mr. Harrington except me," Mr. Wolf grumbled as he speared a fillet and placed it on his plate.

"You'll get to meet him Friday evening. He's picking me up for supper at seven-thirty." Mr. Wolf and Sarah stared at Josephine over her announcement. "I think you'll like him, Papa."

"I'm sure I will if he gets on well with both you and Mathias."

Throughout the remainder of the meal, Josephine caught her father gazing at her often. She'd miss their quiet suppers once Marlene was always there. Marlene expected constant chatter, but the Wolfs were comfortable with companionable silences.

"Josephine, you're a lovely woman," Mr. Wolf said when they stood at the close of the meal. "I want you to go back to Mademoiselle Bisset's shop tomorrow and get another dress for your Friday supper engagement."

"Papa, that isn't necessary."

His arm went around her before kissing her forehead. "It's your birthday month, and you deserve a bit of spoiling."

Josephine hugged him and gave her thanks before they settled in the parlor, she with a crossword puzzle and he with the evening newspaper.

***

On the evening of Friday the thirteenth, Josephine joined her father in the parlor. Mathias conveniently had an engagement of his own and left not long after he'd returned from work.

"Are you sure you'll be all right, Papa?"

"Perfectly content, Jo." He kissed her cheek and looked over her new pale green sheath dress. "I believe I'll enjoy a quiet evening to myself. There won't be many of those left."

Josephine laughed. "Marlene does like to talk."

When the bell rang, Mr. Wolf was quick to his feet. Josephine eagerly listened to everything happening in the entry hall.

"Mr. Wolf, it's a pleasure to meet you, sir."

"Likewise, Mr. Harrington. Please come in."

Dressed in a smart three-piece navy suit with a red cravat, Cyrus looked impeccably handsome. His grin widened the closer he came to Josephine.

"Jo, you're lovelier than ever." He kissed the back of her glove.

"Do you have a few minutes to spare?" Mr. Wolf asked.

"Of course." Cyrus settled beside Josephine and her father took his regular chair.

"Marlene is more than excited to see your plans this coming week," he remarked.

"It's a joy to work with enthusiastic clients, and on a lovely home. This project has me doubly blessed in that regard."

"Mat told me you've been in town for about a month. Are you settling in all right?"

"More than comfortably. I got the keys to my new home yesterday and had it thoroughly cleaned. I plan to spend my spare hours on its decoration as a means of showcasing my abilities."

"How very clever."

"It was Jo's idea. You must be proud to have such an intelligent daughter. The fact that she's beautiful is a glorious bonus."

Mr. Wolf nodded. "I'm very fond of her myself. She has her mother's smile."

"You're blessed to have that reminder."

Josephine stood. "If y'all are done talking about me like I'm not here, I'm ready to go."

Her father came to her to kiss her cheek. "Go easy on him, Josephine."

"I have a feeling Cyrus could handle anything I throw at him, Papa."

Cyrus laughed and offered his hand. "I'll have her home by midnight, Mr. Wolf."

"Enjoy yourselves, Mr. Harrington."

After she donned a new gray cloak, Josephine's father waved them out the door. A Stoddard-Dayton touring car from the Mobile Taxi Co. fleet waited at the curb. Cyrus assisted her into the generous backseat.

"I planned something unconventional," he said once the automobile headed out of the neighborhood. "You did, after all, applaud me for being such."

Smiling, she slipped her hand into his. "That sounds fun."

Cyrus lifted their linked hands, slipped off her glove, and kissed her knuckles with a lingering playfulness. "You always smell wonderful, like a summer afternoon."

"I make my own perfume with lemon balm."

"I adore your earthiness, Josephine."

They stopped on St. Francis Street in front of his new house. With an urbane smile, he escorted her up the stairs and through the front door. After taking her cloak, gloves, and reticule, he brought Josephine to the dining room. The table was laid with a lace cloth and set with fine china, crystal, and silver.

"Welcome to our private dining experience, Josephine Wolf." He pulled out her chair to the left of the head seat, and rang a silver bell once seated.

Two waiters promptly arrived with a wine bucket and covered trays.

"Thank you," he told them. "That will be all."

The waiters bowed and left as efficiently as they arrived. Cyrus opened the wine with practiced ease and poured the red.

They each sipped, watching the other.

"I asked Mathias about your preferred foods before creating the menu. Hopefully he wasn't joking that you eat shrimp."

He lifted a silver cover off the largest tray revealing a lovely dish of de-tailed shrimp in garlic sauce over pasta and steamed zucchini.

"It looks and smells wonderful," she assured him.

"I catered it at the hotel, as I still have my room there through the weekend, and hired the waiters to bring it over during their break."

"It's completely unexpected, Cyrus. I appreciate your thoughtfulness."

"Thoughts of myself, I'm afraid. I wanted uninterrupted time with you, Jo. Mathias is all boisterous jokes, and Miss Jensen clucks nonstop. You appear to be the right amount of wit and fire to fuel my days—and nights." He dished up a serving of everything for her while leaving the innuendo dangling.

"How is it?" he asked after she sampled everything.

"It's seasoned to perfection and the zucchini still has a bit of crispness, which is how I like it."

"I'm glad. Tell me something about you. Something weird and random, possibly shocking."

She chewed and swallowed while thinking. "I was recently reminded that the woman I learned about herbs from was considered a witch by most people."

"And she wasn't to you?"

"She was a kind old woman I met one afternoon in the cemetery."

"The cemetery?"

"I used to go there to play because I was teased so much in the neighborhood."

"And you didn't find it odd she was hanging around the graves?"

"So was I, so no. I often sit on my mother's grave and talk to her."

"Does she ever answer?" His brow rose as he watched her.

"No, never." She held his gaze with a smirk. "Did I pass the test?"

"With flying colors." He winked.

"What about you, Cyrus? What odd tidbit will you share?"

He flashed a mischievous grin. "The tame version or the naughty one?"

"Always naughty when that's a choice."

"I'll do one better." He took another drink from his wine glass. "I'll tell you two truths and a lie. Will you play as well?"

Josephine nodded.

Cyrus leaned toward her, tracing a scrolling design on her bare forearm. "I'm uncoordinated at using my tongue during sexual encounters, I've been with men, and I prefer to sleep naked."

She blinked, staring at the serious set to his jaw. "Am I supposed to guess?"

He trailed his fingers through hers before settling back in his chair. "You can, but I won't confirm or deny anything."

"Well, if you have a faulty tongue, you'll be the first man I know of to be self-deprecating about his sexual prowess."

They locked eyes for several seconds before erupting into laughter.

Once they settled back to eating, her awareness of Cyrus's attentions heightened. He studied her lips, hands—every shift of her body. Coupled with his scandalous declarations, it was arousing as her brain silently worked the possibilities of his truths.

"It's your turn, Jo." Cyrus licked his lips. "What are your truths and a lie?"

Not wanting to be outdone by his scandalous choices, Josephine paused to gather her thoughts. She decided to sandwich the lie in the middle. "I sometime spy on neighbors, I've kissed dozens of men, and my breasts have been devoured by an ardent—though temporary—lover."

"If the last is one of the truths, that's a foolish man to have lost your favor." Blue gaze intense, his tone deepened with his next words. "Josephine, I've wanted you since the moment you walked into the Vineyard Café last Friday. Seeing you on Monday was serendipitous in the fact that it introduced me to Miss Jensen and allowed me the chance to see you again so I could ask you to supper."

Her eyes widened. "You believe in serendipity?"

"Why else would I have met Mathias except to be introduced to you? I felt the pull to accept his friendship though his boisterous behavior isn't my preferred companionship. When I saw your radiance, I knew you were the hidden treasure."

Cyrus's right hand went to her cheek, and he angled closer over the corner of the table. She tilted to accept him, and their lips gently met. It wasn't frenzied, but the passion was there in the way his hand trailed her neck.

When it naturally ended on a note of fulfillment, Josephine smiled. "It's a good thing we're both eating garlic. That could have been awkward."

He smiled and kissed her once more.

At the close of the meal, Cyrus dispersed the remainder of the wine into their glasses and motioned to them.

"If you carry those, I'll get the dessert tray so we can settle somewhere more comfortable."

Josephine followed him to the front room, placing their glasses on the bare coffee table beside the small, covered tray before sitting in the middle of the sofa.

"I might be a fool, and please excuse my ignorance, but I had no idea if you ate cakes and such since they're often made with eggs. I went to the candy shop." He removed the lid and held out the platter. "Take your pick, Jo."

She laughed at the array of colorful confections of spun sugar and candied nuts.

"You're marvelous, Cyrus. Thank you." She plucked a peppermint stick. "This should chase the garlic away for starters."

"I'll never complain about garlic when it's accompanied by you. But just to be safe…" He took one for himself and set the platter down.

Cyrus told Josephine of his childhood in Atlanta. His three older brothers all hunted for fun, which he never enjoyed and was picked on because of it. Two of his brothers were already full partners with their father and the third had created a contracting business so he could be hired to build things for Harrington and Sons. Their differences were inflamed when he wanted to take more personal time for floral design than keep to the family business.

"Only my mother encouraged me," he said. "She was the one who taught me about flowers in her rose garden—the pride of the city. But after the scandal over Labor Day weekend at the country club, she could no longer defend me."

"Do I want to know what happened over Labor Day weekend?"

"Probably not."

"Then you needn't say anything more, Cyrus."

"My father paid me off to discreetly leave town before the press got wind of what happened. I traveled a bit, then decided to put roots in Mobile when an acquaintance mentioned there was a need for tableau and float designers for the Mardi Gras season. Since they both incorporate a bounteous amount of fresh flowers, I felt it a perfect fit."

"I hope it is."

"My drawings were chosen by Order of Mayhem for the tableau, and another society has commissioned me for half a dozen floats. Those plans are being worked on by a painting crew in the float barn already. I'll help finalize things, especially with the florals, before the parades next year."

"That's wonderful, Cyrus. And the interior design will keep you busy in the offseason, though if you wish to get in on the wedding and cotillion seasons, flowers could keep you busy all year." She finished the peppermint stick and rubbed her fingers together. "I can never eat one without getting my fingers sticky."

He took her wrist and kissed her fingertips, nibbling and sucking each finger, his agile tongue cleaning the candy residue.

"Your tongue is in no way uncoordinated, Mr. Harrington."

Cyrus lifted a shoulder without commenting, though there was a slight smile on his lips.

"That means you enjoy sleeping naked and have been with men," she whispered the forbidden words.

He didn't flinch as his deep blue eyes held her gaze.

"But you're here with me now, Cyrus. What do our pasts matter?" she questioned, thinking of her blunder with Sean. "We've all wandered, we've all strayed."

"And your brother said you weren't religious."

"I go to Mass on the main Holy days, but I feel closest to God in nature."

"You incite reverence in me, Jo."

Cyrus's sweet mouth was on hers once again. The moment was pure tenderness. Honest. Josephine knew then that what she and Sean had played at was frenzied lust, even if she'd dreamed of him for over a decade. The only thing that hurt was her pride when she realized Sean wasn't taking her as a serious option.

They drank the wine and she munched honeyed almonds while Cyrus spoke of his travels to New York, Boston, Chicago, and New Orleans that autumn along with the museums, galleries, hotels, and colorful parade of people he had observed. Throughout the hours of the conversation, they migrated along the sofa, sometimes sitting shoulder to shoulder, other times with her legs draped over his, or him lying with his head resting on her lap. The natural ebb and flow of their togetherness thrilled her.

The wine was long gone and the sweets half-eaten when he finally pulled his pocket watch out of his vest. "It's after eleven. The driver is supposed to return at eleven-thirty. We have twenty minutes, then the ride home."

"It doesn't seem nearly enough, does it?"

Cyrus shook his head. "I haven't talked like this in ages, nor have I *ever* felt a connection to someone as I do you. Thank you, Jo. I've enjoyed this night more than I dreamt possible."

She shifted into his lap, arms around his shoulders as she kissed his brow. "You're a beautiful soul, Cyrus. Thank you for this evening."

"Would you dine with me again Monday night?"

"That's my birthday, but I don't think there's a family supper planned, and I'd enjoy more time with you."

They kissed and cuddled the next several minutes, then Josephine checked herself in the washroom, marveling at the spark in her eyes and the healthy blush on her cheeks despite it being so late.

On the ride home, they held hands. It was all so perfect she hardly believed she was awake rather than fantasizing.

Cyrus walked her to the front door. After a chaste kiss on the lips, he smiled. "I'll see you Monday, Jo."

"Goodnight, Cyrus. And thank you, again, for the lovely evening."

She slipped inside and padded up the stairs.

Mr. Wolf's bedroom door was open, his bedside lamp creating a shadow that stretched into the hall. He looked up from reading and raised his brow.

"I had a lovely time and he invited me to dine again with him on Monday. You didn't have birthday plans, did you?"

"No, I was going to ask you what you wanted to do. I could take you to midday dinner instead. I'm glad you have something to look forward to, Jo."

"And how was your evening?"

"Blessedly quiet. Sleep well, my girl. Midnight is already in your room."

Josephine washed and changed for bed. Once lying down, she relaxed into the trance that allowed her spirit to separate from her body. Out the open window she flew. For the first time, her destination was north—St. Francis Street. Seeing Cyrus's house, she circled it before perching on the balcony railing and reminiscing over the amazing evening she'd spent there.

Twelve

After a weekend spent mostly with Cordelia that included a trip to Monroe Park, art supply shopping downtown, and a long visit with Francesca Wilton—who was stuck at home with her invalid mother—Josephine woke on her birthday to Midnight pawing her chest. Stroking his back wasn't enough, so he head-butted her chin to demand more attention.

"You want food, Middy. I understand."

She dressed in the orange walking suit since her father was taking her out for noon dinner, swept her waist-length hair into a loose chignon, and descended the stairs.

"Happy birthday, Jo." Mr. Wolf's mustache wiggled as he smiled.

"Thank you." She stopped at his chair to kiss his cheek.

"Enjoy your day, Jo," Mathias said over his coffee cup.

"I will, Mat. And thank you again for the hat." He had gifted it to her the night before in case she wanted to coordinate her ensemble with it that day.

"Good morning, birthday girl!" Sarah carried in a tray and came directly for Josephine.

Oatmeal with brown sugar, pecans, cinnamon, and raisins was artfully arranged in the bowl Sarah set before her.

"Thank you, Miss Sarah." Josephine hugged her for several seconds. "I love you."

"I had to do something special since you're denying me your birthday supper for the first time ever."

"Our girl isn't so little anymore," Mr. Wolf remarked.

"What's going on tonight?" Mathias asked.

"Jo is dining with Mr. Harrington," their father answered.

Mathias's eyebrows rose. "Again? I wonder why he didn't mention that to me when I saw him yesterday."

"He's meeting Marlene today with his plans for the house. Did he tell you that?" she countered.

"It was bound to happen sooner or later," Mr. Wolf said.

"What?" Mathias grumbled.

"Your sister turning the head of one of your friends. Don't be jealous." He stood. "I hate to rush out, but I want to get to the office early since I'm taking a longer break. I'll be here at a quarter to twelve to pick you up, Jo."

"I'll be ready."

Not long after Mr. Wolf left, Sarah answered the front door. She came back holding a vase of gorgeous orange roses.

"Someone has an admirer," she said as she set it on the table. "And they match your dress."

Josephine's smile froze, and she tore into the little envelope.

I hope your birthday is blessed with everything you want, Jo.

Sincerely, Sean Spunner

"Sean has a lot of nerve to send me flowers!" She tore the note into tiny pieces and tossed them into the fireplace.

"What exactly happened between you two last Monday?" Mathias asked.

Being a week removed from the event made it feel like old news when so much had shifted in her life since then. "We teased each other into action, but I was the bigger fool for thinking he wouldn't be guarded."

Mathias chuckled. "What made you think you could outsmart a man like him? It's said he's the sharpest lawyer in the city. Not to mention he has a decade on you."

"I built him up into this valiant prince, honorable and kind. I didn't expect him to be a selfish cad."

"Welcome to the reality of men, Josephine." Mathias waved his hand. "Just be a good girl, settle down, and do as you're told."

She laughed and grabbed the vase. "That's as likely as Papa becoming a showgirl."

Josephine stalked to the kitchen and set the roses on the counter. "The admiration is officially mine to you, Miss Sarah. I hope these brighten your kitchen."

After breakfast, she was still upset over Mathias's words. Too finely dressed to work in the garden, Josephine did what her outfit was named for—walk. On her second loop around Washington Square, Cordelia ran over with a large package wrapped in brown paper.

"I telephoned, and Sarah said you were out here." She thrust the box at Josephine. "Happy birthday, Jo!"

"Oh, Del, thank you." They took the nearest bench, and Josephine balanced the long box in her lap. "You won't believe who had the nerve to send me roses this morning."

"Not Mr. Spunner!"

Josephine nodded, glad her best friend knew about her foray into the forbidden with Sean, as well as her evening with Cyrus, both of which she had shared during their weekend excursions.

"Mathias was there and finally asked what happened when I went to Sean's house. He tried to tell me all men were like that."

"Can you two still speak to each other like you did as children?"

"Yes, unfortunately. I wouldn't be surprised if he sent messages to interrupt my evening with Cyrus tonight."

"Don't let your broody brother and selfish neighbor ruin your day." Cordelia tapped the unopened present. "Enjoy this surprise."

Inside the wrapping was a two-by-three-foot canvas done in ink and watercolor of Josephine's herb garden in summer. Near the left side was Josephine in a blue dress amid shades of green and lavender with Midnight at her feet.

"It's utterly charming, Del. I love it! Thank you."

The friends were hugging when an automobile pulled to a stop at the curb.

Sean leaned out the open window. "Is the birthday girl giving out hugs or collecting them? I'd happily participate in either."

"The nerve of him," Cordelia whispered as she straightened. "But he looks as handsome as ever."

"Ignore him and walk home with me, please," Josephine whispered back.

They stood as one and cut a diagonal path through the park. Sean followed at a slow pace, looping the block until he parked in front of the Wolf house, forcing them to have to walk past him in order to go home. Josephine handed Cordelia the present and took the lead before crossing Charles Street.

Sean leaned against the side of his automobile, arms crossed, chin high. "I'd like the chance to tell you I'm sorry if I hurt your feelings last week, Jo."

"That's unnecessary, Mr. Spunner, as were your roses."

Cordelia paused beside her, looking him over as though thinking of Josephine's descriptions of him.

"May I have an introduction to your friend?"

"No," Josephine said at the same time Cordelia spoke.

"Cordelia Barnes of George Street." She offered her free hand.

"The pleasure is mine, Miss Barnes." He kissed the back of her hand and flashed a dashing smile. "Barnes… you have a passel of brothers, don't you?"

"Yes, Mr. Spunner."

"I know the oldest two. They're good men."

"And much better behaved than you, from what I hear." She giggled and he blushed.

"Have you heard from your teacher lady?" Josephine asked.

He shook his head.

"Come on, Del." She ushered her toward the porch.

"Jo, please forgive me," Sean called. "I was a tad insensitive."

She nodded and held his golden stare. "And I was filled with lust and deviousness."

"Deliciously so," he said with a lift to his brow and a huge grin.

"As much as I'd fantasized about you for years, Sean, we aren't a good match." Josephine quirked a smile. "But I hope you hear from your science teacher soon."

"Shall we part as friendly neighbors?" He offered his hand along with a disarming smile.

She took it and nodded.

"I loved every moment with you, Jo, from the very beginning. You were a terrific kid who turned into an amazing woman. Don't change, darling. And don't settle for less than true love." He kissed the back of her hand and released it. "Enjoy your birthday. And you have a great day too, Miss Barnes."

"If you ever need—"

Josephine pulled Cordelia into the house before she could say more.

***

Josephine had noon dinner with her father at a seafood restaurant near the river. He seemed distracted, and there wasn't much conversation, but that allowed her to relax, which was needed after the reconciliation with Sean. When he had driven away, Cordelia had followed her into her bedroom and insisted on rehearing everything that had happened between them. Cordelia's takeaway from the whole ordeal had been "I think I'll grab his backside next time I see him, so I can know for myself how tight it is."

Josephine shook her head thinking about it now.

"What is it Jo," Papa asked.

"I was reminiscing how everything has changed this month—even my relationship with Cordelia."

"Is she jealous of the attention you're getting?"

"Not exactly, but she does yearn for something of her own."

"I always thought she would be a lovely daughter-in-law." He sighed. "I fear Mathias will never be interested in settling down. He is so different than I was at his age, though I love him and am proud of both of you."

Once home, Josephine changed into old clothes and went to the yard. Midnight found a sunny spot on a flagstone while she trimmed and weeded the kitchen herbs to keep busy. Thoughts of Cyrus filled her mind. She hadn't seen him since Friday night, but knowing Mathias had spent time with him over the weekend gave her an odd dread. Mathias hadn't announced when he would be moving into the downstairs apartment, but she worried for Cyrus's peace when that happened.

She stayed in the yard until sundown, then washed and dressed for supper. The formal affair called for her new white underset and the sage gown trimmed in gold. In practice for the masquerade, she pulled on the above-the-elbow silk gloves since she had never worn a pair that reached beyond her wrists.

When Josephine descended the stairs, she brought the painting from Cordelia to show her father.

"It's lovely," he declared. "Just as you are."

The doorbell rang, and he leaned it against the coffee table before answering.

"Come in, Mr. Harrington."

"Call me Cyrus, please, Mr. Wolf."

Josephine stayed on the sofa when they entered, smiling over Cyrus's crisp good looks in a black tuxedo.

"Happy birthday, Jo." He briefly kissed her cheek before sitting. He immediately reached forward to lift the painting.

"That's Cordelia's gift."

"She captured your essence perfectly. Would you trust me with this, Jo? I'd like to have it framed so it will be a focal point in your room after the changes are made."

"Yes, thank you."

"Where will you be dining tonight, Cyrus?" Mr. Wolf asked.

"I have a private dining room reserved at the Cawthon. It's become a bit of a second home to me, even while settling into my house. Being only a block away, I can easily dine there until I acquire a cook." Cyrus stood. "I'll have Jo home by eleven, Mr. Wolf."

While they traveled in the hired automobile, Cyrus cupped her cheek and held her gaze in the dim light of the backseat.

"I'm pleased to spend this special evening with you."

"And I'm thrilled to be with you, Cyrus." Her hand went to his knee, and she leaned in for a kiss that lasted the remainder of the ride.

The private room was resplendent with wood trim framing the murals and a modern light fixture with an inverted pyramid centered above the round table in the middle of the room. Their chairs were placed only a foot apart before the exotic flowers that perfumed the space with desire.

The massive carved credenza, extra chairs, and china display cabinet along the walls were ignored in favor of Cyrus's profile as he nodded an unspoken instruction to the maître d'.

"You look amazingly happy tonight, Jo. I'll be selfish enough to say I hope a smidgeon of that is over being with me."

"More than a smidgeon, Cyrus."

He fingered her smile lines before leaning in for a hard kiss.

Afterward, he rested his temple against hers and whispered. "Do you crave more, Jo?"

"Yes, so much more."

Grinning, he trailed her neckline with a teasing touch. "Soon enough."

Josephine nodded to the flowers. "The arrangement is lovely."

"I'm glad you think so. I saw to it myself before I picked you up."

The meal began with a fragrant vegetable soup and finished with dorado fish steaks grilled to perfection.

"I thought we could walk to my house and spend the remainder of our time there."

"That sounds fine," she said, laying her napkin on the table.

At the coat check, Cyrus discreetly kissed Josephine's neck when he placed the cloak around her. A trail of heat coursed from the location to her middle. She flashed a flirtatious smile which he returned.

Josephine respectfully held his arm on the westward walk down St. Francis Street. As they approached his house, she noticed a dark figure sprawled on the front steps.

"Cyrus and Jo!" Mathias slurred and then lunged at them.

Springing in front to catch him, Cyrus stopped her drunken brother from slamming into Josephine.

"Have you no shame?" Cyrus asked.

"Says the man who's bringing my sister to his house without a chaperone."

"May I call you an automobile to get you home?" He sat Mathias back on one of the bottom steps.

"I thought I could crash here."

"Absolutely not," Cyrus snapped.

"If you let me move into the dungeon—"

"I told you yesterday it will be after the first of the year before it's anywhere close to being ready. If you want out of your house so badly, you'll need to find another location."

"How about some coffee?" Mathias tried to take his hand, but Cyrus shook him off.

"You can drink it at home, though I suggest going to bed." Cyrus looked at Josephine. "I'll telephone for a ride. Would you like to wait inside?"

"What about our automobile to get home?"

"It's supposed to arrive at ten-thirty."

"I can wait." Mathias tried to stand but stumbled.

Discouraged over her brother's state, Josephine sighed and turned to Cyrus. "Rather than use two cars, I'll go home now."

"Baby sister is going to help her big brother! Someone loves me, Cyrus, even if you don't."

Josephine flinched at the pain in her brother's voice.

"I'll be back in a minute." Cyrus disappeared inside.

Josephine leaned against the banister at the bottom of the steps as several men headed down the sidewalk towards them. "What is going on with you, Mat?" she whispered.

"I looked for you at all his regular places. I couldn't find y'all, but I bought a drink at each location." His voice was unnaturally loud in the dark.

"Why go to that trouble?"

"We've never not had a family supper on a birthday. I wanted to join you."

"A birthday! Is the Witchy Wolf of Washington Square finally of age?" Edgar Melvin was one of the men in the group that was passing and he stopped while the others continued. "I don't recall her ever being presented to society."

Before Josephine could speak, Mathias wobbled to his feet. "Jo's been of age, Edgar, and you know it."

The other men from the group turned back to watch.

"But no one would want her, would they?" Edgar said with a vile smirk before his growing audience. "Dirt under her nails and venom in her veins makes for an ugly girl no matter the age."

"Hey, Edgar, knock it off," one of the men said.

He brushed aside the hand that was placed on his suit sleeve and sneered at the man. "Looks like Witchy Wolf got you under her spell already."

Mathias fell to his backside on the stairs, causing the men to chuckle.

Hazel eyes blazing, Josephine went toe to toe with her old tormentor. "Schoolyard tactics are unbecoming, especially for adults. It's time to grow up, Edgar."

He laughed as Cyrus's front door opened behind them. "What, do you think I should have changed my opinion of you over the years? You're still a filthy witch, with or without a new dress."

"Excuse me, gentlemen, but I'll not have speech like that at my front door." Cyrus said as he passed Mathias, who was leaning his head against the iron banister.

Edgar took in Cyrus's tuxedo and precise manners. "Excuse me, sir. Maybe you weren't aware of the riffraff on your steps."

"I only see a man having a poor night, and my supper partner who is suffering under your ungentlemanly conduct," Cyrus replied.

"Perhaps you don't know better," Edgar said, "but the Wolf siblings aren't the type you want to get involved with."

"I'm perfectly capable of choosing my companions, thank you."

One of Edgar's buddies clapped him on the shoulder. "Give it a rest, Ed."

"I think you should listen to your friend and continue to your destination," Cyrus said as he trailed Josephine's silk glove to caress her hand before bringing it to rest on his forearm.

Edgar sneered but held his tongue. His friends nodded to Cyrus and wished them goodnight before continuing down St. Francis Street.

"You should have punched him like you've done before, Jo," Mathias said with a laugh.

"I didn't want to get blood on my dress," she said with a smile.

"Have you really fought him?" Cyrus asked.

"Shall I give you the two truths and a lie version of my childhood?"

Cyrus shook his head, but his mouth relaxed into a grin. They waited for the automobile side-by-side. When it arrived, Mathias was put in first, then Cyrus handed Josephine in. When he started to climb in behind her, she touched his hand.

"You don't have to accompany us."

"I want to make sure you get home safely." Cyrus closed the door and leaned to her ear as the car pulled away. "And I want my promised time with you, Jo."

Pleased with his honesty, she leaned against his shoulder for the duration of the ride.

Mr. Wolf was still in his study when they returned. He took Mathias upstairs—practically by the ear. "Public drunkenness is not acceptable, especially when it isn't Mardi Gras. If Hammel's finds out about something like this, you could lose your job."

The words faded as they turned a corner upstairs.

"I'm sorry about that, Jo," Cyrus said. "I had a feeling he'd do something stupid after our conversation yesterday went sideways."

She settled beside him on the sofa in the parlor. "If Mathias is everything you want to escape, why were you looking for a house with him?"

"I came across him in Bienville Square my first week in town, and he attached himself to me. Not knowing anyone, I thought it would be good to have a local's eye when I looked at real estate. Mathias took it upon himself to find a place we might both fit at. I didn't want to potentially offend him by refusing outright. Looking back, I see that was a mistake. I hope to legitimately stall the downstairs apartment with renovation issues so he'll find a place elsewhere."

"But why is he so clingy with you? I've never known him to be like that."

"He saw we have something in common, but it's not as similar as he thinks. I don't mean to be cruel, but after all I've gone through these past few months, I can't be strung into someone else's search for happiness and keep my own intact. It's still too fresh for me."

Josephine nodded. Though she didn't understand everything, she trusted Cyrus would explain it all in time. She laced their fingers together.

"Jo," Mr. Wolf said from the stairs. "Could you please see to the lights and door after Mr. Harrington leaves?"

"Yes, Papa," she called back. "Goodnight."

"Goodnight, Jo. I'm sorry your birthday had to end on a sour note. Thank you, Cyrus, for getting my family home."

"It was my pleasure, Mr. Wolf."

"But not the drunk Mat and Edgar Melvin parts of it," she whispered.

Cyrus searched her face as they listened to her father's retreat. They both seemed to hesitate, then their lips met.

For the next hour, Cyrus and Josephine held each other. She shared her experiences with Edgar and the other bullies from her youth, but more often than not, they silently watched the fire in the hearth while cuddling. He left at ten-thirty with Cordelia's painting and a promise to collect Josephine Wednesday night for another supper out.

Thirteen

Over the next week and a half, Josephine and Cyrus spent most of their evenings together as well as the majority of Saturday and Sunday with Vaudeville shows at the Lyric Theater, long walks, an afternoon at Monroe Park, and meals out. Plus, unknown to him, Josephine made sure Cyrus arrived home safely each night. St. Francis Street was her new haunting ground during her astral wanderings.

Mr. Wolf accepted Cyrus as an undeclared suitor and had him included in their holiday plans. Cyrus and Marlene were both over for Christmas Eve, and they were all to go to the Jensens' house for Christmas dinner the following day. In the leisurely hours between supper and Mass, Josephine and Cyrus played chess in her father's study to hide from Marlene's constant chatter about the redecorating that was to begin the day after Christmas.

Mathias perched on the arm of Cyrus's chair and plucked the cigarette from his lips.

"Mat," Josephine said, "we're trying to concentrate on the game."

Her brother took a deep drag from the pilfered cigarette and exhaled a smoke ring. "What am I supposed to do at a time like this when everyone is paired off?"

She caught his haunted gaze. "Do you want to sing Christmas carols or play charades?"

"What am I, seven?" He laughed. "How 'bout a drinking game?"

"No thank you." Cyrus stood and crossed to the fireplace, fingering the collection of timepieces on the mantel. "Would you like to go for a walk, Jo?"

"It's too damp for that," Mathias said.

"You don't have to come," Josephine said, "but the fresh air might do you good."

"Good for what?" He puffed on the cigarette.

"Jo is trying to be helpful," Cyrus spoke with force bordering on anger. "Be grateful you have a sibling who cares about you, especially at Christmas."

Mathias rolled his eyes, smashed the cigarette into the ashtray, and left the room.

"Cyrus." Josephine breathed his name before burying her face against his chest as she hugged him.

"I'm all right, Josephine. You've made the heartache of being away from my family bearable."

He kissed the top of her head, then down the side of her face until he was in line with her mouth. Josephine felt Cyrus to her soul with the deep kisses that followed. His hand low on her back pressed her further into his embrace. When their lips separated, he rested his head on hers. He swayed ever so slightly as though they were moving to the music of their hearts.

"I never believed I'd meet my soul's match," he whispered, "but here you are."

They stayed entwined until Mr. Wolf found them.

Josephine excused herself to make hot chocolate for everyone. It was her favorite holiday treat because she associated it with her mother. Sitting on Mrs. Wolf's bed the Christmas Josephine turned five, she and Mathias drank cocoa from their mother's fancy teacups as she read the story of Jesus's birth from the Bible while their father sat in front of the fireplace. To her, that was the heart of Christmas: something sweet in the belly, a good story, and the ones you loved around you.

When they left for the cathedral, Marlene sat beside Mr. Wolf on the front seat. Josephine was squeezed between Mathias and Cyrus in the back, their coats making the ride extra warm during the frosty night.

At the Cathedral of the Immaculate Conception, Mr. Wolf led the way up the steps with Marlene on his arm. The portico was crowded with Christmas well-wishers seeking to display their holiday best.

"Shall we find a seat?" Cyrus asked.

Josephine nodded, but before he could bring them through the doors, Marlene snatched her arm.

"Josephine, come say hello to Mr. and Mrs. Stuart and my dear friend, their daughter, Kate. She's always one of the first to sign up for charity functions. Stuart family, this is Jesse's daughter, Josephine, and her friend Mr. Harrington. He's the one that's going to make over Jesse's house. You'll have to come see it. And Mathias. Don't be shy. Everyone, this is Jesse's oldest."

Cyrus was polite but didn't offer open-ended commentary, which helped them pass through the gauntlet of curious faces. After pausing long enough for Josephine to don a white mantilla, they escaped into the nave. He led them a third of the way between the pillars beneath the arched blue ceiling and claimed the end of the pew on the main aisle. He draped their outerwear over the back before they settled.

Mathias, who had stayed with them, sat on her other side.

"He moves fast, doesn't he?" her brother asked.

"Who?"

"Your Mr. Spunner, but she's not nearly as elegant as you, Jo."

Eyes following her brother's gaze, Josephine watched the short, curvaceous brunette on Sean's arm. She wore a plain blue walking ensemble, which could have been Sunday best for a teacher, but they both glowed with love. They went almost to the front, joining the Finnigans in the pew they always claimed.

"They look happy," Josephine remarked.

"So do you," Mathias said with dejection, then crossed his arms.

Mr. Wolf and Marlene settled on the pew in front of Josephine minutes before Mass began. The rumble of the organ and the heavenly pitch of the choir stirred her soul. She clasped Cyrus's hand. He smiled before closing his eyes as though absorbing the music.

Then Mathias reached out in anguish.

God, I'd deny my sister nothing, but why taunt me with this?

She looked at her brother. His dark lashes were down over closed eyes, fingers knotted as though in penitent prayer as the organ vibrated the pew.

I can't damn her, my own sister, but him…. I've never wanted another more than I want him. Either give him to me or send him away. I can't stand to see him touch her, be so gentle with her, when I want nothing less than his unabashed passion.

Josephine gasped.

Mathias's olive complexion visibly paled as he turned to her, realizing she had heard. "Jo—" his whisper began, but she fled.

Down the aisle between the pews she raced, her mantilla long gone before she reached the portico. Josephine blocked Mathias's mental calls, refusing to hear any excuses for his honest plea.

Her feet tried to revolt against the dainty boots, but she dashed through the patches of light the streetlamps provided against the festering dark. She raced toward the river first, zigzagging through alleys and backtracking through the shadowed streets.

She ran for an hour, then slowed but continued a westward course through deserted neighborhoods until she collapsed against the cemetery gates. Closed but not locked. As soon as Josephine entered, the tears flowed. Half blind, she staggered through the grid of death until she found the correct section.

At her mother's plot, she collapsed and hugged the frigid base of the angel statue.

"Mama…Mama. How could I have been so ignorant? Cyrus told me at our first supper that he had been with men. Was Mathias one of them? Did Mat have a claim on him first?"

Chest heaving with sobs, she clung to the granite as she fell into the abyss of pain.

Dew drops coated Josephine over the next hour. Closer to dawn, the layer of damp turned to ice crystals. But still she clung to the symbol of her mother.

"You were right for us to check here again, Cyrus," Mathias said from the darkness.

Josephine sought to hold tighter to her anchor, but she couldn't move.

Someone fell to his knees and rubbed her shoulders.

"Jo, my dearest Jo. I'm here to take you home." Cyrus pried her fingers from the angel. "She's frozen, Mathias. Run ahead and telephone for a doctor. Have your father bring the automobile, but I'll start carrying her."

Mathias left as Cyrus put his coat around Josephine. Then his hot lips were on her, attempting to fill her with life.

"Stay with me, Jo." Cyrus cradled her as he started for the gate, keeping a steady pace under the inky sky.

There was an automobile, then the familiar scent of her father's tobacco when she was carried inside. Marlene and Sarah undressed her, dried her hair, and put her in her warmest flannels before tucking her into bed with hot water bottles at her feet.

Sometime later, Dr. Moore poked around, checking her eyes and throat, then asked questions.

Too heavy and cold to speak, Josephine lay in suspended disbelief as her father explained that she had run out of Mass and had been missing for hours without a cloak in the elements. The doctor gave instructions for her care and left.

How could she continue to live in bliss when she and Mathias loved the same man? Josephine turned her face toward the wall and willed the tears to stay inside.

"At least she's out of danger," Mr. Wolf said. "Allow me to take you home and so you can get some sleep, Marlene."

"But what of Christmas supper?"

"I'll stay with her." Reliable Sarah.

"With Sarah staying, Mathias and I could come to your parents' this afternoon as planned. Cyrus too—"

"I'd rather stay and help Miss Sarah with Jo," Cyrus stated.

"Then that keeps your numbers even, Marlene."

Mr. Wolf kissed his daughter's cheek, and the rustle of Marlene's satin dress marked their departure.

"You better get some sleep, Mathias," Sarah told him.

Another soul left the room.

"And you, Mr. Harrington—"

"I'm not leaving her today."

"Bring in the wingback chair from the guest room, and I'll get you a pillow and blanket."

"Thank you, Miss Sarah. I appreciate it more than you'll know."

"You don't get to be my age without understanding how things are between people. Thank you for getting her home, Mr. Harrington. Miss Jo has had things rough and is independent, but she needs you even if she never admits it."

"In the few weeks of knowing Jo, I can honestly say my life will be hollow if she's not in it."

There were comings and goings, but Josephine kept her eyes closed, hoping the darkness would return.

A minute later, four paws dropped on the bedspread beside Josephine's right shoulder. Midnight's nose bumped her cheek, his whiskers tickling her jaw. Her mouth twitched with a smile.

"Your cat, Jo. He'll bring you comfort and extra warmth."

Then Cyrus's lips were on her forehead. "I wish I knew what pained you, but even if you don't want to talk about it now, I'm here for you."

Midnight curled onto her torso, and Cyrus settled beside the bed in his borrowed chair. Josephine wasn't sure which brought more comfort, but she was able to sleep.

***

The smell of peppermint roused Josephine from slumber. Without thinking, she looked around. Cyrus immediately leaned over.

"There are those gorgeous eyes. Don't try to move if you aren't ready to, Jo." The mint was from his mouth. She yearned to kiss him—until she remembered.

131

He rang the silver dinner bell that was on the side table and Sarah appeared.

"Miss Jo, at last! What can I do for you?"

She requested to use the bathroom. Sarah saw her there and back while Cyrus waited.

"Are you hungry, Miss Jo?" she asked once Josephine was tucked in bed. "It's going on noon."

She rubbed her hands beneath the covers to try to alleviate the stiffness. "Yes, and thirsty. Would you use my healing blend for a cup of tea?"

"Of course, Miss Jo. You'll stay with her while I fix a tray, Mr. Harrington?"

"Certainly." Cyrus promptly returned to the bedside chair and reached a small tin box out of his jacket pocket. "Mint?"

She nodded.

"I tend to eat a lot of them when I can't smoke." He smiled and retrieved one. "Open your mouth, and I'll place it on your tongue."

She accepted it, then rolled to face away from him. His hand rested on her shoulder in a caressing motion that made her shiver.

"Do you need another blanket? Midnight went downstairs with Miss Sarah, but I could go look for him."

She shook her head.

When Sarah returned with the tray, Josephine insisted she stay. Seeming to understand her plea, she turned to Cyrus.

"Why don't you go home for a while and freshen up, Mr. Harrington? Mr. Wolf and Mathias will be here until three, but you can be sure I'll stay with Miss Jo, no matter what."

His concerned gaze held Josephine in its azure spell several seconds before she nodded.

"All right then." He sighed and stood. "Merry Christmas, Jo. Miss Sarah."

"Merry Christmas, Mr. Harrington."

Josephine slowly drank the vegetable soup and tea. Only when Sarah took the tray and stopped at the bedroom door did she speak in an authoritative way Josephine had rarely heard since childhood.

"He loves you, Miss Jo, and he's good for you. Don't let your stubborn pride get in the way."

"But you don't know what—"

"You've been over the moon for him these past weeks. I don't see how he could have offended you in the cathedral to make you turn your back on him."

"Miss Sarah, I'm sorry you had to work on Christmas," she said in an attempt to change the subject.

"This isn't work for me. As soon as I got the telephone call that you were missing, I rushed over. There's nowhere I'd rather be than with this family. Now be true to Mr. Harrington and yourself, or I'll be chasing you with a switch like I had to do with Mathias when he was a boy."

Josephine's body tensed at the mention of her brother. Sarah frowned but left without further word.

Her eyes were closed, and she was in bed, but there was nothing restful about it.

Mr. Wolf came and went without trying to rouse Josephine. Later, Midnight settled on top of the blankets beside her legs.

And then he came.

I know you aren't asleep, Jo.

Mathias took the chair and fished her closest hand from beneath the covers. She tried to pull away, but he held firm.

I'd forgotten how the cathedral amplifies your abilities. I never would have…you didn't deserve to find out like that. I'm sorry.

Why didn't you tell me, Mat? You should never have introduced me to Cyrus without telling me you had feelings for him.

I know, but you never knew about my preference. Will you still love me even though I hid this side of me from you?

She nodded, lips tight. "As long as you're open from here on out. I won't judge you, Mat. You should know that by now."

He grinned. "You're a peach of a sister. Cyrus loves you, Jo. Don't allow my feelings for him to stop you from expressing yours."

Cyrus appeared from the hall wearing a fresh charcoal suit and red bowtie.

"I don't know what I just walked in on, Jo, but I can assure you Mat and I never—it hasn't crossed my mind to be anything but a friend to him, and even that was done with caution." Looking at Mathias, he continued. "I tried to discreetly tell you on several occasions that you and I are different."

"What can I say?" Mathias shrugged. "I'm stubborn."

"I've always loved who I loved, man or woman, and have been in relationships with both. But Josephine, you're the only one with whom I've been open about this. With my past relationships, I played whichever side to fit the circumstances. I wanted you to know from the start. You knew, and you didn't turn away. Please remember that."

Josephine nodded solemnly.

"Tell me honestly, Cyrus," Mathias said. "I know I pushed myself on you, and I'm sorry about that, but do you want me to rent your apartment?"

His angular jaw shifted. "Whoever rents the apartment needs to understand I'll be running my business from the home. Whatever happens on the property has the potential to reflect on me. Respectability would be of paramount importance."

"How diplomatic of you to phrase it that way," Mathias said.

"Mat, are you ready?" Mr. Wolf asked from the door. Seeing his daughter awake, he came in. "Jo, my girl. How are you feeling?"

Mathias moved to allow their father to sit.

"A bit better. I'm sorry for causing concern. I didn't think—I just escaped."

"I didn't realize your mother was still such a big part of you. Are you upset over Marlene joining the family?"

"It's not Marlene, Papa. I've always gone to Mama's grave when I'm worried about something."

"But you're okay now?"

"I believe so. Have a lovely time with the Jensens and tell me all about what I missed when you return."

"I will, Josephine." He kissed her forehead and looked at Cyrus. "Make sure she has a good Christmas."

"Yes, sir."

Once they were alone, Cyrus perched on the edge of the bed and stroked Midnight while gazing at Josephine.

"May I massage your hands?"

"Yes, please. They're stiff. I drank my soup rather than using the spoon."

Cyrus kissed the back of the hand, then the palm, before gently rubbing from the center outward.

"That feels wonderful, Cyrus. Thank you."

He nodded and smiled. "Tell me what the connection is between you and Mat. How did you know what was going on with him during Mass? I didn't hear anything."

That's because he was speaking without talking out loud, she said with direct focus on Cyrus.

His blue eyes widened.

Kiss me on the left cheek if you can hear me.

He did so and she smiled.

"How are you communicating like this?"

Josephine told him how she and Mathias had developed the ability during their forced quiet times. "I can get others to hear me, but he can only talk to me. I'm stronger with it than he is. The cathedral magnifies it like a conduit, allowing me to hear him when he isn't actively seeking communication."

"I'd like to try to learn."

"I'd love for you to know, but it takes time and uninterrupted practice."

"We'll make it work, Jo."

Sarah came to the door. "How's our patient doing, Mr. Harrington?"

"She's in better spirits, Miss Sarah," Cyrus answered as he continued to massage her hand.

"Should I fix some coffee?"

"That would be nice, thank you," Josephine replied. *When she's gone, Cyrus, I expect a thorough kissing. We'll have at least five minutes alone.*

He grinned and leaned close as soon as Sarah went for the stairs.

Fourteen

The day after Christmas was Thursday. Cyrus arrived at the Wolf house at eight in the morning along with two workmen to start on the guest room. He stopped in Josephine's room long enough to greet her with a kiss before removing his suit jacket and rolling up his sleeves.

Forced to stay in her bedroom for one more day of rest as the doctor ordered, she listened to Cyrus conduct the preparations for wallpapering the space. Curious, Midnight came and went before settling on the square of sunlight near Josephine's window.

"What is all that noise?" Cordelia asked when she breezed into the bedroom the next hour.

"The redecorating has officially begun." Josephine held out her arms. "Come sit with me, Del."

She shifted over so Cordelia could prop against the pillows with her.

"Miss Sarah said you were out all Christmas Eve night, took poorly, and have to stay in bed. She's going to bring us tea in a little while."

"I'm doing fine today, but you know how she worries."

"Does the decorating mean Cyrus Harrington is here?" Cordelia whispered.

Josephine nodded.

"I can't believe you've been selfish enough to hide him from me all these weeks. Where is he?"

"Watch and see."

A man went by the open door carrying a side table.

"Him?"

"No, just wait." Josephine smiled, hoping to see Cyrus again herself.

The other worker in overalls passed, and she shook her head before Cordelia could ask.

When Cyrus stopped in the doorway, Josephine waved in welcome.

"If you have the time, Cyrus, come meet Cordelia."

He took Cordelia's hand and kissed the back of it. "Thank you for being such a friend to Jo. I've wanted to tell you I admire your talent. Jo allowed me to take your painting so I can frame it for her."

"How thoughtful, Mr. Harrington."

"Please call me Cyrus."

"It's a romantic name," she simpered with a flirtatious smile.

"And so is Cordelia." He came around to Josephine's side. "Your coloring has improved. I'm glad to see that, but I must get back to work as I only have the morning before going to the staging area for the tableau this afternoon."

She nodded and he kissed her hand slower than he had Cordelia's. They watched him leave, then turned to each other at the same time.

"He's gorgeous!" Cordelia hissed.

"I think so."

"But he isn't flashy like Mr. Spunner."

"He's humble and introspective—two things I appreciate."

Sarah delivered the tea tray. "Will you be staying for dinner, Miss Cordelia?"

"I need to attend a gathering of the sisters-in-law and aunts with my mother. The women always take dinner together the day after Christmas."

"That's lovely," Sarah remarked. "Mr. Harrington has accepted my invitation to have dinner with you, Jo. I'm sure your father would approve of you coming downstairs to eat."

"I feel more than up to it," she said. "Thank you for inviting Cyrus."

"I knew you would appreciate it." Sarah left with a huge smile.

"I wish I could stay, but I can't break a family tradition for a handsome face that isn't looking at me the way Cyrus looked at you," Cordelia said.

"And how was that?"

"Like he wanted to bundle you in his arms and devour you."

"I wish he would."

"Have you told him about your powers?" she whispered.

"The telepathy, yes, but not the spirit wanderings, though I have been using it around him without his knowledge."

"Are you spying on him at home?" Cordelia's eyes lit with intrigue. "Have you seen him disrobed?"

"I make sure he gets home safely. Sometimes I sit on his balcony and observe the night sounds of the city."

"I wonder how he'll compare to Mr. Spunner when you discover more of him."

They laughed and talked, earning green-eyed glares from Midnight when they got loud enough to disturb his rest.

An hour later, Cordelia stood.

"Come visit me tomorrow. We could stop next door and tell Francesca about your Cyrus since you refused to the last time. She needs cheering up after my brother dropped her. She's living off your herbal teas, you know—one to function during the day, and the other to help her sleep at night." Cordelia picked up the tray. "You've been doubly blessed with attentive men this month while the two of us on George Street are withering away. We'll live vicariously through your stories. I'll bring this to the kitchen on my way out. Goodbye, Jo."

Josephine spent the next hour fantasizing about Cyrus—how his body would feel, the way they'd move together, the taste of his skin. She ached at not knowing a more intimate experience with him than she had shared with Sean, but realized the intimacies with Cyrus went deeper. They were connected in a way that outshone physical desire, even if she yearned for his touch as well as his conversation.

The man himself stopped in the bedroom doorway, his suit jacket restored. "I'm here to escort you to the dining room."

"Where are your workers?"

"Gone for their break. They return at one-thirty to begin papering. I'll check the progress this evening."

In her rush to get to him, Josephine hurried out of bed. The room spun as she stood. Cyrus's arm went around the waist of her flannel nightgown and hers around his neck. Without hesitation, their lips met. Their kisses were long and deep as the room continued to spin. Seeking balance, Josephine pressed her body to his.

His breath hitched and he clutched tighter. "Not now, Jo. I want you, but we must be patient."

"I'd wait forever for you, Cyrus." She rested against him, soaking in his peace.

His hands roamed her back and he kissed her hair. "I've been in and out of relationships since I was sixteen, but they haven't all involved sex. I haven't been free with my love or casual in my morals except this past Labor Day weekend when I allowed myself too much indulgence."

"That makes me feel special."

"You are special, Jo. I'll cherish every experience with you all my days." His left hand traveled her side then outlined her unbound breast with a tentative caress.

"Don't make me come up there, y'all!" Sarah hollered from the bottom of the stairs.

With a giggle, Josephine shifted away from Cyrus.

"We'll be there in a moment!" she called while retrieving her robe from the bench at the foot of the bed. Cyrus helped her into it and left a sweet kiss on her lips.

In the dining room, Sarah gave them a silent appraisal when she delivered the soup, bread, and cheese.

When they were alone, Josephine caught Cyrus's gaze. "I worry about Mat being reckless. I'm bad enough, but he can be worse."

"I hate to say it, but it might take a scandal to shock him into change."

"He's had a bit of heartbreak already," she said with a frown.

"I was only ever cordial to him, Jo. I never led him on."

"I'd never think that of you. It's just he's been too needy to be understood that he's grasping at anyone he thinks might be sympathetic."

Cyrus sighed. "I can't help him. I don't know enough people here or how things like this work in Mobile."

"Lives out of the norm are ignored by polite society if they're kept quiet. But I worry about his drinking. He loses all sense of decorum when he's drunk. The night of my birthday is a prime example of that."

Cyrus nodded. "I understand and will offer helpful reminders, but that's all I can do."

***

By Friday evening, the guest room was papered in a metallic floral design with elements of the orient in its bold gold background with exotic flowers. The new furniture pieces would be delivered on Monday from Easton and Sons, an import company and furniture warehouse.

"It's truly a statement, isn't it," Mr. Wolf remarked when he arrived home and found Josephine and Cyrus studying the completed walls.

"That it is, Mr. Wolf."

"After seeing this, I wonder what Marlene has planned for our bedroom."

Cyrus laughed. "I've promised not to disclose details, but I have managed to rein Miss Jensen's ideas into choices that will please both of you."

"He's brilliant, Papa."

Mr. Wolf chuckled and stroked his mustache. "He likes you, Josephine. That's enough to prove his intelligence in my books. Allow me to dress for supper. Please entertain Marlene if she arrives before I'm ready."

She assured her father she would, watched him leave, and then took Cyrus's hand.

Cyrus shifted closer with a sensual grace that was magnified by the spark in his eyes. He wrapped her waist with both arms as he nibbled her neck.

"Would you run away with me?" she whispered.

"Temporarily, after I finish the tableau. I need to be able to provide for us, Jo. I'm sorry if it's not romantic."

"On the contrary—that's the most romantic thing of all. You're putting aside your cravings for my long-term benefit. I love you."

He stared, surprise changing to wonder as his gaze softened. "I love you too, Jo. Everyday my feelings for you strengthen, but I haven't wanted to say the words in case you weren't ready to hear them. Thank you for being brave."

"I want to share everything with you, Cyrus. I yearn to explore your body and spend hours in your arms, naked and free."

He kissed from her jaw down her neck, taking advantage of the scoop of the blue dress's neckline.

Is that really such a good thing to be doing right now? Mathias asked.

Josephine looked at her brother in the doorway. *It feels great to me.*

Cyrus slowly lifted his head to follow her gaze. "Excuse us, Mat."

He absently nodded as he looked around the space. "The room looks good, Cyrus."

"Thank you."

"Are you staying for supper tonight?" Josephine asked.

"Yes, my final Friday night supper here. I'm moving next week. I found an apartment above a shop on Dauphin Street. It even has a balcony overlooking the road, which will be perfect for Mardi Gras parade viewing."

"Wonderful, Mat!" She hugged him. "You look pleased."

"Pleased to be free to be myself. Are you still going to the Order of Mayhem ball?"

"Of course."

"I didn't know if you would since the benefactor is"—he made a rude gesture—"with that lady he brought to Christmas Mass."

Josephine snorted. "It's none of my concern what Sean Spunner does. Besides, I'm not turning down my first chance at a masquerade, especially when it's Cyrus's debut tableau and the man I love is bringing me."

Mathias looked between them with a bittersweet smile. "I'm pulling an initiation stunt for my society that night."

"I hope it isn't something too shocking."

"Wait and see, Josephine." He tweaked her nose and smirked. "But first we have a family supper to get through."

Fifteen

Mr. Wolf left in his hired automobile to collect Marlene for the New Year's Eve ball, leaving Josephine alone to wait for Cyrus. The rich purple of the dress fabric gave her skin a lustrous glow, or perhaps it was thoughts of Cyrus. They had spent some portion of every day together since Christmas, marking another week of enhanced emotions within their growing relationship.

"Jo?" Cyrus called as he pushed open the front door that was not completely closed.

"I'm in the parlor."

She smiled as he looked her over and crossed the room to him. Cyrus touched the velvet trim on the silk gown without hesitation. His hands spanned her hips, tugging her closer until his lips brushed hers. The kiss dropped to her collarbone and finally the swell of her breasts at the square neckline.

"You're beautiful, Jo," he said as he straightened.

Then their lips were searching, tongues teasing as they embraced.

"I wish to stay in your arms all night, Cyrus." She fingered his white bowtie—precisely tied as always—and dreamt of mussing his perfect hair with her gloved hands as they tumbled together. Then she inspected the gorgeous boutonniere with a deep purple rose as its centerpiece. "Did you do this?"

He nodded.

"I love your talent and eye for beauty as much as I do you."

"And I love you, Jo, but we have to arrive on time." He turned for the door. "Which cloak are you using?"

"The black one. And my mask is on the credenza. It matches my gown."

He draped the covering around her shoulders and tied it at her throat before retrieving her mask.

The automobile ride to the Battle House Hotel allowed enough time to discuss how they spent their separate afternoons—Cyrus overseeing the final touches in the ballroom, and Josephine puttering around the garden.

Cyrus, wearing a black satin mask that coordinated with his tuxedo trim, pocketed her coat check ticket and presented their invitations at the door to the Crystal Ballroom. Josephine feasted on the elegance as he led her through the throng of guests. Opulent purple drapes pooled the ground wherever they hung, and the irises and roses that matched his boutonniere in the flower arrangements were touched with gold on the edge of their petals, creating a shimmer of magic when you walked the room.

"It's gorgeous, Cyrus. The flowers are sumptuous and the gilt embellishments the height of sophistication."

"I'm glad you approve." He kissed the apple of her cheek below her mask. "I only wish my mother could be here to see this. She taught me everything I know about floral design."

"Was the room photographed before guests arrived?"

He nodded.

"Then send her some photographs. It won't be the same as her experiencing it in person, but I'm sure she'd love for you to share your accomplishments with her."

He clasped her hand. "Thank you, Jo. Thinking of you here with me was part of what kept me going this week between all the projects."

Josephine gave him a curling smile. "What did you imagine us doing?"

"Something exquisitely naughty between the columns over there." His lips brushed her ear with the whispered words. "As a matter of fact, that would be a good place to stand while the Order of Mayhem members make their entrance. Wait until you see the boutonnieres I designed for them."

When the fanfare began, Cyrus led them to the shadowed space reminiscent of a Greek temple. He wrapped his arms around Josephine's waist and settled close behind her. The masked revelers unofficially commissioned to begin the Mardi Gras season paraded into the ballroom in a choreographed line. Rather than small boutonnieres, the members in front had elaborate arrangements that included giant bird feathers that marked them as leaders within the group. Josephine thought she recognized the gray head of Mr. Finnigan with an ostrich plume and Sean's strut towards the middle of the group.

Once the parade was over, Cyrus and Josephine circled the room before she located her father beside Marlene who was in a gold dress. They were surrounded by the Jensens, Stuarts, and a few other couples. Soley on appearances, Mr. Wolf fit in with the group because his tails were tailored by the best shop in town, but it was odd for Josephine to see her father in the thick of the season's revelry after his years alone.

"Mr. Harrington, do come here with Josephine!" Marlene called and then hooked her arm through Josephine's. "You look lovely. Jesse said you did, but one never knows how objective fathers are. And Mr. Harrington, the man behind this amazing display. I don't recall anything quite so tasteful at a masquerade in the past decade. I know you'll be the savior of the Wolf household as well. It's only been a few days and the guest room is transformed into the glorious Far East. He'll be the talk of Mobile, Mrs. Stuart. You must schedule him now before word gets out and he's booked through the next carnival season. Mr. Harrington will leave me cards, and I'll bring them to the next bridge party."

"Now, Marlene," Mr. Wolf said. "The young people didn't come to talk business—they wish to dance. Allow them to go."

"I'm not so old, am I, Jesse?" she quipped. "Take me dancing too."

Mr. Wolf and Marlene made it to the dance floor before Josephine did, which was fine by her. She didn't want her future stepmother seeing too much of her dancing. Josephine was sure she didn't have the finishing school refinement in her waltz steps, though Mathias had taught her the popular dances over the last several years.

As though sensing Josephine's unease, Cyrus asked, "How about a drink first?"

"Thank you."

They had champagne, which she drank too fast. Cyrus took the lead and they were soon spinning around the floor. It was easy to feel graceful in his arms. His stance was of someone with plenty of practice, but she didn't begrudge his years of experience because he was with her now.

The next hour, the string quartet left the stage and a ragtime band took over. The energetic music enlivened the ball and caused the youngest masqueraders to fill the floor with cake walks, bunny hugs, and the turkey trot.

In the middle of a turkey trot, someone pulled Josephine away from Cyrus. Turning to the new partner, Josephine met Sean's proud grin. His eyes were shadowed behind the mask, but she could tell there was a twinkle in them.

"You're glorious, Jo." Feet keeping the beat, he hugged her closer. "And your tits look scrumptious."

Josephine smirked and fingered Sean's boutonniere. "I see you ended up with the perfect feather. A grackle for Sean Spunner—the flashiest crow, but intelligent and attracted to shiny things. I suppose my chest is glowing like pale moonlight."

Sean's laughter turned heads. "You're fire, Jo. I hope Cyrus Harrington isn't easily burned."

"He's tougher than he looks." Josephine smiled as the tune ended. "Thank you for the invitation, Sean, and remembering the promised dance. I hope all is well with your teacher."

"Hattie and I couldn't be better, that is unless we were upstairs in one of the hotel rooms." He winked. "Allow me to bring you back to your escort."

Sean complimented Cyrus on the tableau and praised the boutonnieres before retreating.

Cyrus kissed Josephine's temple as he settled beside her at the table, sitting sideways in his chair. "Mr. Spunner is as smooth-talking as one would expect from a lawyer."

"I wouldn't claim his speech skills too highly. He blurted that my tits looked scrumptious while we were dancing."

They laughed and Cyrus's arms went around her so he could nuzzle her ear. "I look forward to tasting more of you, Jo. Shall I collect another drink for us?"

"Yes, please." Josephine watched him cross to the refreshments, and then let her gaze roam over the dance floor.

Mathias was turkey-trotting with a solemn-looking brunette in navy blue. She was graceful enough, but it pained Josephine to see her brother looking bored.

Try to smile, Mat. She isn't that bad of a dancer.

His head angled up, masked eyes scanning the crowd until he smiled at his sister. *She's the sister of one of the other pledges. He asked a few of us to dance with her because he fears she's going into spinster territory. She's your age, Jo.*

You're hilarious.

Edgar Melvin, his red hair a beacon without a hat to cover it, was in conversation with another man at the edge of the dancing. As though feeling eyes on him, Edgar looked around. Catching Josephine's gaze, he grinned. She frowned and forced herself to look away from him but felt his approaching vileness.

"You're still hanging onto Sean Spunner like you did as a little girl," Edgar said as he crossed his arms. "Does the new man in town know of your history with him—how he would fight your battles and ride you around town like a cherished pet?"

"That's none of your business," Josephine snapped.

"But I think it should be Mr. Harrington's business, seeing as how he's spending all his leisure hours with you."

Cyrus returned with their drinks, his cool gaze raking over Edgar. "Aren't you the man who harassed Jo a few weeks ago outside my home?"

Edgar smirked. "You still haven't seen through her, have you?"

"It's none of your concern." Cyrus handed Josephine her glass, then gently took her elbow to lead her away.

"You're not the first to be bewitched by her," Edgar said when they were a few steps away.

Cyrus turned back. "I'd think poorly of the men in this town if I was."

They didn't stop until Cyrus brought Josephine to a quiet alcove. He studied the guests for several minutes while they sipped the wine.

"I'd say he has an interest in you," Cyrus said, "but I see his eyes on Mathias more often."

"He's pestered us both for nearly all my life, but I don't wish to think of him anymore. I'm here with you, Cyrus. You have my undivided attention."

A few minutes later, Mathias was back in her mind.

Don't worry too much when the Mystics of Dardenne prank begins. Out of respect for Cyrus's work, I talked the others into toning it down.

Mat, explain yourself! she mentally yelled, but he didn't respond.

When the next tune ended, the lights flickered off. There were a few screams, then the electric chandeliers came back on in the center of the room. Four men in tight red devil costumes ran onto the dance floor. The outfits included masks that covered their heads completely, obscuring their identities, but Josephine knew Mathias was the tallest one.

"Order of Mayhem no longer deserves their name!" one of the devils shouted.

"Mayhem includes debauchery and chaos!" another shouted.

Several ladies shrieked but there were also a few catcalls.

Two of the devils ran through the room, grabbing at women and taking them on sensual dances through the aisles, but Mathias and the others welcomed four costumed newcomers that arrived with buckets in each hand and bottles of champagne. Sharing their load, the buckets of water were tossed at those who wore the biggest boutonnieres. Tables were drenched, tuxedos and dresses dripped. Champagne bottles were partially chugged, then splashed around as well.

Buckets empty, the devils each ran for a different exit. Edgar Melvin stuck out his foot to trip Mathias as he ran by. Always light on his feet, Mathias was upright within seconds and able to clear the nearest door before he could be apprehended.

I'm glad you were able to escape, Mat, even though Edgar tried to stop you. All those years running bases paid off.

Be sure to tell Cyrus I did the best I could to save his tableau. We were supposed to use red wine.

"It's such a waste," Cyrus lamented as he eyed the nearest soggy centerpiece.

"It was supposed to be red wine," Josephine said as she held his hand. "Mathias talked them down so it wouldn't interfere as much with your design."

"It's still an immature stunt for grown men to do at a gathering like this."

"Welcome to the madness of Mardi Gras." Josephine kissed his cheek. "You more than make up for their shenanigans with your cultured display of decorations and manners."

The band started playing and the guests slowly returned to their previous activities.

When the lights next dimmed it was for the approaching midnight hour. As the countdown began, Cyrus led Josephine into the privacy of the columned space. In their little temple of love, he stared into her eyes as the crowd counted around them.

Five. Four. Three…

Their lips met to the sound of noisemakers and shouts of "Happy New Year" and "Happy 1913," but while the hoopla faded to nothing, their heated embrace continued.

Sixteen

On the night of Friday, January third, Josephine was stretched the length of Cyrus's sofa with her hair unbound. They had dined at the Cawthon and walked to his house afterward on the pretense of him showing her the masquerade photographs he had chosen to send his mother.

He set the pictures on the coffee table and leaned back against the sofa from his seat on the floor beside Josephine.

She trailed her fingers through his hair as she spoke. "Your mother will love them, Cyrus. After all you've told me about her, I know she'll be even prouder of you."

"That means a lot, Jo." He went to his knees, smiling at her. "I was glad to be with your family over Christmas and staying busy this past month kept me from missing her as much as I would have otherwise. Hopefully working on the other rooms at your house and the float designs in the coming weeks will keep me sane as well."

"Why don't you invite her to visit?"

"I wouldn't be much of a host with all my work, and the guest rooms upstairs aren't ready yet."

"The hotel is within walking distance, Cyrus, and I would be happy to show her around Mobile." She kissed him. "Think about it."

Cyrus nodded, a thick wave of hair falling over his forehead from Josephine mussing with it. His sad gaze turned soft and he trailed a fingertip over her lips.

"You're more beautiful that any flower arrangement, Josephine." He gently knelt on the edge of the sofa and lowered a kiss to her mouth. "You smell sweeter, and I'm certain you're rose petal soft everywhere."

"Why don't you find out?" she asked as she shifted seductively beneath him. His hand trailed under her skirt.

"Jo," he whispered as he caressed the flesh above her stockings. "There's not enough room on here for what I want to do with you."

"Then bring me to your bed."

Josephine hadn't been upstairs since the original house tour the month before. The front bedroom was much the same though the four-poster bed was gone. In its place, a curving brass bed draped in blue stood romantically.

Cyrus unbuttoned his shirt. Josephine stepped into his arms as soon as it was removed. His skin was warm and soft with a sprinkling of hair on his chest. Hands roaming across his torso, she kissed from his jaw down until she was on her knees before him.

"Jo, I don't want you to be subservient to me. We're equal partners in pleasure. I will never force you to do anything you don't want to."

"But I thought you might like—"

"What I like is to see pleasure on my partner's face, hear it in their voice, and feel it with their climax." He removed her shirtwaist and corset as he spoke and then brushed her waist-length hair behind her shoulders. "Josephine, I want you to be my partner for the rest of my days. Our first joining will solidify our relationship and it needs to be an amazing experience for us both."

"It already is, Cyrus."

While they kissed and touched, they undressed until they were skin on skin. Josephine shivered at the sensation of their naked embrace.

"I adore your freckles." Cyrus kissed her shoulder where a grouping of them dusted her pale skin. "All of them, but these are my favorite. They remind me of constellations in the summer sky."

"I've never felt like this before," she whispered.

Hands trailing every curve, Cyrus guided her to the bed. He lowered her beneath him and explored with a gentle hand. "You're beautiful, Josephine. Thank you for sharing your body with me."

His intimate touch continued as his hungry kisses roamed.

"Cy!" she gasped and responded to each stroking movement with an echoing motion.

He feasted more before shifting into place with his velvet touch. Sighing in surrender, she felt him to her soul with their complete joining. After a tender kiss on the mouth, they moved in tandem toward their mutual goal. There was too much happening to understand it all, so Josephine focused on Cyrus's face—the burning passion in his eyes with the divine promises of undying love.

"I'm getting close, Jo." Cyrus slowed. "Do you want me to pull out?"

"No, never." She linked her hands around his back.

"But it could mean you get with child."

"I want to mother your children, Cyrus Harrington."

When their lips met, he rolled over so she ended up on top. Josephine marveled at the way he touched every part of her. He leaned forward to kiss her throat, causing more electricity to pulse through her body. She kept moving long after Cyrus found his release because the sensations were too pleasing to quit until she could no longer support herself.

Wrapped in each other's arms, her head rested on his chest. She listened to his heartbeat slow as her mind sought to reconnect with her body.

"That was the most exquisite experience of my life, Josephine Wolf."

She kissed his chest and smiled though he couldn't see her face.

"Are you all right, Jo?"

"I'm full—full of love, wonder, and you. I never want to lose this connection. It's only been a month, but I love you in a way I never thought I was capable of."

"I feel the same. Do you genuinely want to have a child with me?"

"We'll nurture any babies that come from our actions."

"Then you'll marry me, Jo?"

"I'd marry you right now if I could."

"It might be better to wait at least a month."

"Better for whom, the high society clients you plan to woo? I suppose we need to think of your career so you can support our children. I'm sure there will be a lot because I never want to *not* do what we just shared."

Cyrus laughed and hugged her tighter. "We can announce the news to your father, and then plan the ceremony before I write to my mother."

"A simple wedding outdoors."

"Wherever you'd like, Jo."

They were quiet for a while, Cyrus trailing his fingers on her back.

"I'm glad you got a new bed. I don't like thinking of the man who last used this space. I know you had the house cleaned, but would you mind if I burned white sage the next time I come? It has cleansing and restorative properties. It's good to use after someone is sick or when there's been a lot of change."

"Do whatever you wish to make our home comfortable for you, Jo." He sat up enough to look at the clock. "The car will be here in half an hour. Do you want to shower before you dress?"

"No." She kissed down his torso, her hair sweeping across his body until she stopped at his navel. Looking up to catch his eye, she smiled. "I want to go to bed with your fragrance on my skin and dream of you all night. Let's use our final minutes in more productive pursuits."

Knowing what to expect with the second coupling, every part of her was immediately open and wanting.

Cyrus kissed her spine after his release. "You're glorious, Jo. What we have is beyond anything I ever imagined. If I had known, I would have waited for you."

She turned to him, hand on his cheek. "None of that, Cy. Everything you've been through has made you who you are today. I wouldn't trade this version of you for anything."

They kissed and caressed longer than they had time for. After they dressed, they hurried to the waiting car.

"How do I look?" Josephine asked as she patted her hasty chignon.

"Like you've had amazing sex," he whispered so the driver wouldn't hear.

She smiled and took his hand. *It was amazing, Cyrus. I didn't know my body was capable of all that—the giving and taking. I feel alive on a level I've never experienced before. I want to taste more of you and witness you climax in every possible way.*

"Oh, Jo." His hot mouth was on hers the rest of the journey.

The downstairs was dark, and Midnight waited on the steps when they reached the porch.

"Papa must have gone to bed already, but I'll tell him about our engagement when I see him."

Cyrus nodded. "Sleep well, Jo, and telephone me tomorrow."

They parted with a savory kiss.

Midnight followed Josephine into the house and took the lead upstairs. The small chandelier that hung in the middle of the stairwell guided her across the now unfamiliar path of her childhood. Pausing in the middle of the steps that spanned between the two landings where the stairs took ninety-degree turns, Josephine looked down on the nook where she used to read to her dolls. Now she could only imagine Cyrus there. He was her past, present, and future.

She practically floated to her room, but one word brought her back to earth.

"Josephine?"

"Yes, Papa." She went to his open door. Only a small side table light was on, and he was propped on his pillows. Maybe he wouldn't notice her unkempt hair, darkened lips, or the heat still on her skin from the sexual flush.

"How was your evening with Mr. Harrington?"

"Wonderful. We're—"

"Mr. Milligan was back in the office today. He works in receiving, but has been in Atlanta since Christmas, visiting family. We took our luncheon together, and he told me all about Georgia's society crowd, glad that I was marrying a sensible woman from Mobile."

"That must have been nice to hear."

"No, it wasn't." He sat up, clasping his hands over the bedspread at his waist. "He told me some of the rumors that went around in recent months that his family was still chattering about. One story involved a member of Harrington and Sons. How many architectural firms in Atlanta do you think there are by that name?"

She shifted back a step. "One, I imagine."

"You're right. And of that one architectural firm, how many men by the name of Cyrus do you think worked there?"

"One." Josephine breathed the word.

"How do you think I felt to learn the man who is decorating my house and courting my daughter—"

"Not courting, Papa. We're engaged. Cyrus and I are going to marry." She approached the foot of his bed in her excitement.

"Mr. Milligan's cousin was at the country club Labor Day weekend with the fast crowd. Apparently they broke in after hours to keep their revelry going and…" his words slowed as though weighing how much to share, "things got wilder in the early morning hours. I can't allow my daughter to marry a man with no regard to the law or basic morals."

"That wasn't the true Cyrus. He doesn't drink like that anymore and there were other stimulants involved, Papa."

His eyes narrowed, looking harsh in the dim light. "You don't understand what type of light this puts him in, Josephine."

"I understand that Mr. Mulligan's cousin was caught in a scandal and wanted to deflect the blame. He did that by telling a sordid tale about someone else rather than confessing what *he* was doing at the club."

Her father shook his head. "Don't be blinded by his good looks. Cyrus Harrington isn't who he says he is."

"Cyrus is exactly who he says he is because he's told me everything. He's been honest about his past, where he is now, and what he sees in the future. He's a beautiful, talented soul, and we love each other. We don't need to explain things to strangers or even well-meaning family members to move forward together."

Mr. Wolf shook his head. "I can't allow that."

"I'll leave right now if you truly mean those words, Father. Cyrus is everything to me. I'll not break our bonds over hearsay and half-truths from his past life."

"You have no bonds to him, Jo. You've only known him a few weeks and there is nothing officially announced."

"We're already knitted together. An announcement may be sent to the newspaper because we would like to wed within the month." She turned for the hall.

"Do you know what you're doing?" he called out after her.

Josephine turned back. "I've seen your happiness with Marlene and accept her in our lives because you love her. Can you not do the same for Cyrus?"

Her father frowned and rubbed his chin.

"You've proclaimed my intelligence, now it's time to trust my judgment. Don't listen to rumors spoken by people you don't know. Listen to those closest to you. Marlene adores Cyrus and I love him. See for yourself the type of man Cyrus is by his actions and words. You've dined with him enough times to know he's a gentleman."

He held her gaze for several seconds. "All right, Jo. Have him see me this weekend. I won't send the paper anything until I speak to him. And if I don't approve at the end of the interview, I'll not publicly announce my support."

She nodded at the fairness of his declaration. "Thank you, Father."

Rather than go to her room, she returned to the main floor. At the wall-mounted telephone in the kitchen, she asked the operator for Cyrus's house.

"Hello?"

"Cy, my father wishes to speak with you tomorrow. Come any time, but the sooner the better."

"Are you all right?"

"Yes and no." She paused, not knowing if the switchboard operator was listening during this typically quiet time of the night. "But it's important you come."

"I'll be there, Jo. Goodnight, my love."

Josephine locked herself in her room, stripped off her clothes, and climbed into bed. Hugging a pillow to her naked breast, she fantasized she was holding Cyrus until she was calm enough to astral project.

For the first time, Josephine found his balcony door open to the winter night. Cyrus sat on the rumpled bed, shirt and shoes removed. The light from the hall shone off the brass frame, beckoning her into the space she had left the hour before.

"Jo…" he sighed her name with a smile and lifted one of the pillows, seeming to inhale.

Cyrus, your devotion means everything to me.

"Josephine?"

Yes, you're hearing me.

"But how can you hear me?"

I'm with you in spirit. Another ability I have is separating from my body. I often wander at night, most recently to check that you get home safely, but I've never seen your balcony door open before. I'm glad to be able to revisit the scene of our recent passion. She stopped at the foot of the bed.

"Your lemony scent clings to my linens like the sweet whisper of a dream. May I see you—hold you again?"

Not now, though I'd give anything for another hour with you. As happy as I am, I need to warn you of what I couldn't over the telephone. She settled on the bed beside him.

"You're near, aren't you, Jo?"

Close enough to see the goosebumps on your arms. Be sure you close the door after I leave. I don't want you to catch a chill.

"What are you worried about?"

Josephine told him about the conversation with her father. *I don't know how much Mr. Milligan told him about the party, but he was upset. He might know you were with a man but couldn't admit it aloud. What will we do, Cyrus?*

"I'll talk to your father in the morning and tell him as much of the truth that's needed for him to understand my feelings for you."

Even if he doesn't accept you, I'll come to you, Cyrus. I'm never giving up this connection we have. She gazed at him in the half-light, noting the way the shadows outlined his chiseled jaw and the slim contours of his chest she had so recently kissed. *I love you, but I must return. Communicating with you while outside my body is fatiguing me quicker than I thought possible.*

"Be careful, Jo. I'll see you in the morning, my love."

With a glowing smile she hoped he could feel, she floated through the door and flew home.

Seventeen

"What happened to you, Miss Jo?" Sarah asked when Josephine came downstairs for breakfast Saturday morning.

Josephine smiled, images of Cyrus filling her mind. "Can't a woman be in love without people questioning everything?"

"Certainly, but there's something different about you today." She left the toast rack on the table beside the butter dish.

Mr. Wolf took his seat as Sarah returned with the coffee.

"Doesn't Miss Jo look different today, Mr. Wolf? She looks more mature, even if she still gives me the evil eye."

Josephine chortled, and then colored under her father's studious gaze.

"Perhaps," he said noncommittally as she placed his omelet before him. "Thank you, Miss Sarah."

Once they were alone, Mr. Wolf picked up his fork and pointed it at Josephine. "If that man has made advances toward you, I'll not have him in my house."

"Cyrus would never force me into anything."

He cleared his throat and gave her one more look—almost a glare—before tucking into his breakfast.

Her father's gruff silence made Josephine miss Mathias, who was probably sleeping off his Friday night bender in his new apartment. The only thing worse than the awkward silence at the table would be Marlene trying to make conversation around it.

After finishing her toast with blackberry jelly, Josephine poured another half-cup of coffee.

"Are you in the garden today?" Mr. Wolf asked.

"For a bit. I need to check the herbs drying. Darla Adams comes on Monday."

"Is she still your only customer?"

"My only regular non-tea customer. I sell when the neighbors come asking but enjoy gifting the herbs and teas when I have an overabundance."

"You might need to put more stock into it as a business if you plan to make a go with that man."

"Papa, how can you say that when you've seen Cyrus's work? Once people in this city know what he can do for a house, masquerade, or even a wedding or funeral, they'll flock to him."

"You never know how things will go when a scandal is on the wind."

She left without asking to be excused.

Going through the kitchen, Josephine exited the back porch and went to the shed. The bunches of herbs strung across the ceiling were ready for packaging. The work kept her mind from stewing on her father's harsh words.

Two dozen bundles were weighed and wrapped in cheesecloth before she thought to look at the time. She stepped inside the kitchen, straining to see the clock from the door.

"Mr. Harrington has been in the study with your father for half an hour," Sarah said as she cleaned dishes.

Josephine hurriedly stuck her hands in the scalding sink and washed them. Taking the offered towel from Sarah, she hesitated at the closed study door. Should she interrupt? No.

Cyrus didn't need to be mollycoddled. Besides being capable of expressing himself, he knew exactly what he was walking into. She took the chair in the stair alcove so she would be nearby when they emerged.

It was over fifteen minutes before the door opened. Mr. Wolf looked stern, but Cyrus's grin doubled when he saw Josephine stand. Before he could reach her, Mr. Wolf stopped him with a hand on his arm to come to her first.

"Forgive my harshness, Jo, but as my daughter, your wellbeing is my greatest concern. I'll pen the announcement and send it to The Mobile Register. One of the ship inspectors has a brother who is an editor there. I think I'll telephone Mr. Paterson and see if his son would function as courier this afternoon and deliver it directly to his uncle."

"Thank you, Papa!" She hugged him and he kissed her forehead.

"Cyrus will take loving care of you. I wish you both well and will pay for whatever wedding ceremony you wish. Marlene might take offense that you're getting married before her, but you plan it on your timeline, Jo."

"She'll probably appreciate not having to share the house when she moves in. This can be your honeymoon nest."

He took her hand. "Don't rush out if you aren't ready."

"I'm ready, Papa."

He forced a smile. "You're all grown up now, my girl."

"I'll still love you, Papa." She turned to Cyrus. "But we're both ready, aren't we?"

Cyrus's arms went around her. "Completely ready."

"I don't see a reason to put limits on your visits, Cyrus. You're welcome anywhere."

"Thank you, Mr. Wolf."

Josephine and Cyrus went up to her room. Taking her father's message to heart, she settled on her bed and patted the spot next to her.

"I don't think that's a good idea."

"Just to lounge and talk." She pointed to the door. "I didn't even shut it all the way. I'll behave."

He removed his suit jacket, pushed the pillows against the headboard, and took a reclining position facing her.

"He knows we've had sex, Jo. That's why he's not barring me from your room, but I wouldn't be comfortable making love when he's home." He linked their fingers. "He asked about Labor Day weekend—and, yes, he heard I was with a man. I confessed enough to show my humility, but I didn't tell him all my past like I've told you. He respects my honesty, sees my dedication to work and you, and understands I'll do everything needed to give you food, clothes, and shelter, no matter how modest."

"That's all I need Cyrus. Those basics and you."

Her lips caught his with a playful urgency that caused her hands to grasp him closer.

"Jo, the door."

Laughing, she snuggled into his chest. "So much for behaving."

"Why don't we discuss a wedding date? After I finish Mathias's old room would be ideal. I could take a few days off before needing to start on the float preparations."

Josephine collected her datebook from the desk and returned to Cyrus. "When will Mat's room be done?"

He pointed to January tenth. "Next Friday."

"Where will you bring me for our honeymoon?"

"Across the bay."

She caressed his smooth cheek. "Fairhope or Point Clear?"

"The Colonial Inn in Fairhope sounds quaint."

"I'd like that." She pointed to January fifteenth. "The middle of the week in the middle of the month. Three nights away and then a couple of nights to settle in with you at the house before you return to work. I'm afraid your balcony and porches will become a witch's garden."

"There's nothing better I'd like to see, Jo." Cyrus gave her a nibbling kiss. "A week and a half can't come soon enough."

***

The engagement announcement ran in Sunday's Society page. It wasn't tucked into the middle or off on a lower side—it was the lead tidbit.

> *Jesse Sloane Wolf of Washington Square is pleased to announce the engagement of his only daughter, Josephine Helena, to Cyrus J. Harrington. Mr. Harrington, recently arrived in our fine city, was seen with Miss Wolf at the Order of Mayhem New Year's Eve ball, for which he designed the tableau. A private ceremony will be held for the couple on January fifteenth.*

While Josephine studied the declaration at the breakfast table, the telephone rang.

"Mr. Wolf, Miss Jensen is on the line." Sarah said.

Her father took the telephone in the kitchen, allowing Josephine to hear his side of the conversation through the open door.

"I see no issue with the announcement, Marlene." A pause.

"I'm sorry you feel that way, but it wasn't meant as a slight. Jo *is* my only daughter right now, and I didn't think your name needed to be included since we aren't married yet." Another pause.

"You have nothing to be concerned about, Marlene. I'll see you at Mass."

With a sigh, he hung up the receiver and returned to the table.

"She has a jealous streak," Josephine remarked when her father took his seat.

"And Lord help me!"

They laughed and finished eating.

Mr. Wolf patted her shoulder on his way out. "I'll see you this afternoon, Jo."

Knowing her father was having dinner with the Jensens after Mass, Josephine had told Cyrus she would come over after breakfast. She refused his offer of a hired automobile, wanting the walk to think over more ideas for their ceremony.

"The soup will be in the icebox, Miss Jo," Sarah told her when she came to clear the table. "Heat it on the stove and warm the bread for supper. It's quiet without your brother, but it does lighten my load since you and your father aren't particular about meals, especially when you dine elsewhere for one. Are you sure Mr. Harrington will feed you dinner?"

"Quite sure, thank you. And he's sensitive to my preferences."

"The house will feel empty when you leave. I won't know what to do with myself without your sass or that cat running about."

Josephine hugged her. "I love you too, Miss Sarah. Thank you for mothering me all these years."

"You and Mathias have been my own dear ones. I'd do anything for you both."

Josephine smoothed her gray walking suit and collected her purse, key, and hat. From the shed, she took a woven bundle of white sage off the drying rack and tied it inside a cotton knapsack that she looped over her wrist with the small purse. Midnight received a good scratching and she admonished him to stay in the yard.

When passing the Finnigans' house on Palmetto, Sean ran down the front steps.

"A moment of your time please, Miss Wolf!"

She turned to him. "And for what do I owe the honor of your attentions this morning, Mr. Spunner?"

He laughed, flashing his boyish grin. "I wanted to offer my congratulations over the news that was printed."

"Thank you."

She moved to turn away, but he took her hand. "I'm engaged as well, but our wedding won't be until June. It appears we both move quickly when we see something we want. You met Mr. Harrington the same day I met Hattie." He leaned in conspiratorially and looked her over with his golden eyes. Voice low, he smiled with the question "How was it for you?"

She yanked her hand free.

"You're glowing with the aftermath of a woman well-pleased, Jo. I hope I prepared you properly for the experience."

"It's always about you, isn't it, Sean?" She tried to glare at him but ended up smirking "Our little exploration was nothing compared to what I have with Cyrus."

"Good." His grin was as arrogant as ever. "That's how it should be. You and I are more alike than you want to believe, Jo. Enjoy every intimacy with Cyrus Harrington, but remember who set you off first." He winked.

"You're a real jackass, Sean Spunner."

"I love you too, darling."

Josephine walked away to the sound of him laughing.

The church-going traffic on Government Street was heavy, but she crossed without issue and zigzagged northeast, skirting the cathedral and continuing to St. Francis Street. The first thing she noticed about the red brick home was Cyrus sitting on a new swing suspended from the haint-blue porch ceiling.

"I love it!" Josephine hurried up the stairs and sat beside him.

"I figured you'd appreciate a place to rest while gardening. I have an assortment of terracotta pots arriving this week, as well as some hanging baskets. I want you to choose the necessary substrate and soil."

"This will be a romantic place to sit together in the evenings. And the living screen of greenery will make it private too."

"I'm glad you're pleased, Jo." He kissed her temple and nuzzled her ear.

Inside, she removed her bags, hat, jacket, and boots. Josephine nudged the shoes aside as Cyrus hung her outerwear on the coat tree.

"I have the sage. I'll start the burning in the kitchen." They moved down the hall. "Sarah told me to be sure you feed me dinner while I'm here. I assured her you would."

"We could walk over to the hotel and—"

She shook her head. "I want to taste every inch of *you,* Cyrus."

A gleam in his blue eyes made him look dangerous for a moment.

"*After* I cleanse the air, that is. If you could close the downstairs windows and open those on the top floor, I would appreciate it."

As soon as he left to see to his task, Josephine removed her clothes. In nothing but a full-length camisole, she found a crystal bowl to serve as an ashtray and lit the white sage bundle. She made a slow procession around the kitchen before heading to the front. The dining room and study were seen to before Cyrus descended the stairs.

His arms went around her middle. "You're a magical goddess, Jo."

"I don't want to drop the bowl," she warned as his touching increased.

He set the bowl on the coffee table and swayed against her as their lips met. Josephine worked his buttons open, wanting to feel his skin.

When his shoes and shirt were off, she picked up the bowl.

"You don't play fair, Josephine." Cyrus said as he followed her up the stairs.

She carried the burning sage around the back bedrooms. Cyrus quietly watched from the hall and removed his pants. When she entered the bathroom, he followed. Gently taking the crystal, he set the bowl in the bathtub and stood her before the mirror that spanned the wall between the pedestal sink and the door. They were both fully reflected in their underclothes. Cyrus settled close behind, the heat of his body creating dampness in her core.

"Watch, my love, and see how radiant we are together."

At first, Josephine held his gaze in the mirror as he looked over her shoulder. Then she followed his roaming hands, observing the way she came alive with his touch. When her underclothes lay on the floor, Cyrus kissed every inch of her. His sensual tongue laved, his fingers caressed, and his words stroked a fire until she was nearly panting.

"Those pouty lips of yours are my undoing, Jo." He carried her to the bed and laid her down.

"The sage."

"I'll get it."

Cyrus set the bowl on the still empty revolving bookcase.

"I can sense a change in the air," he said as he joined her on the bed. "Thank you for bringing the sage."

Josephine's hands trailed his warm body. They further explored the ecstasy they shared until both were sated.

"I'm famished." Josephine tightened her leg that was over his hip. "But I don't want to leave this glorious bed. Is it always like this, feeling more in love afterward? Have you felt like this before, Cy?"

Cyrus smoothed her hair and kissed her shoulder. "I thought I had, but compared to these experiences with you, they were shallow. You're my one true love, Josephine Helena Wolf."

They washed and dressed at leisure, and then walked to the Cawthon Hotel to dine in the top floor cafe where they first met. Cyrus was greeted by several regulars who congratulated him on the engagement announcement.

The dinner of blackened crappie and salad took the edge off Josephine's hunger, but she craved more time with Cyrus.

"Would you bring me home on the scenic route?" she asked.

"Which way is that?" Cyrus placed his fedora on and offered his arm before heading for the lobby doors.

"Through some of the parks between here and there, as well as the Wiltons' house."

"It would be my pleasure, Jo."

They crossed Conception Street and settled on a bench facing the fountain in Bienville Square. When the man selling small paper bags filled with peanuts made his way through the Sunday visitors, Cyrus passed him two pennies. Josephine immediately opened the bag, cracked one of the shells, and held the broken peanut toward the sidewalk. A squirrel ran over to collect the nut from her.

"I love the way they quiver their tails," she remarked. "Don't tell Midnight, but I think squirrels are adorable. The ones in Washington Square always get on his nerves because they gang up on him."

Cyrus laughed. "Poor Midnight. Maybe he'll prefer being a city cat."

"I'm worried about his transition." Josephine tossed a peanut to a shy squirrel that watched from around the trunk of a nearby tree. "Be sure you talk to him often when you come over so he gets more used to you. And remind me to pen a letter to your mother when I return home so you can include it with yours. I want her to feel welcomed if she can make it—either for a visit or the wedding."

As the afternoon advanced, Josephine and Cyrus took the streetcar west to reach the Washington Square neighborhood. In the park there, they claimed the only empty bench on the Chatham Street side.

"Will you miss it here?" Cyrus asked as he linked his fingers through her gloved hands.

"I'll miss the green views and trees, but I was harassed so much in my childhood that I don't have any pleasant memories of playing here."

"My dearest Jo." Cyrus kissed her cheek. "We've both had growing pains throughout life, but we have each other now."

The gate at the corner house across from the park opened and Merritt Graves exited along with her husband and a sleek long-haired pointer. Josephine freed her hand and waved to the couple, who crossed the street to them. She often swapped herbs for Merritt's satsumas in the fall, but Merritt purchased the herbs throughout the year when she needed them for cooking.

Josephine and Cyrus stood.

"Congratulations!" Merritt passed the dog's leash to her husband and hugged her neighbor. "I'd be pleased to be introduced to your fiancé."

"Of course. Cyrus, this is Merritt and Bartholomew Graves, and the most admired dog in the neighborhood, Velvet. Merritt is a skilled seamstress and Bartholomew owns a general store just beyond the streetcar loop on the west side of town. Merritt and Bartholomew meet Cyrus Harrington. Cyrus, they've been neighbors since I was running round with scraped knees and who knows what else."

Merritt laughed. "I did have to patch you and your clothes up a few times, Josephine. I'll miss you and your herbs, but I'm pleased for you both."

"Telephone whenever you need something and I'll bring it. We'll be up on St. Francis. Cyrus already made plans for the transportation of my garden. That will be my biggest challenge this month. Hopefully it will flourish by spring."

After more small talk, Mr. and Mrs. Graves continued their Sunday stroll. Josephine then brought Cyrus to George Street to meet Francesca Wilton.

When Francesca opened the door, Josephine jumped into her arms.

"Fran, I had to bring Cyrus over. Cyrus, meet my oldest friend, Francesca Wilton. She's seen the best and worst in me throughout our childhood."

"I can only imagine the antics," Cyrus said with a grin. "It is wonderful to meet you, Francesca."

Francesca invited them into the parlor and then hurried to the kitchen to fix a refreshment tray.

"I made tea with one of Jo's herbal blends," Francesca announced when she returned.

"I've never tried one of her teas," Cyrus said as he accepted a cup. "Thank you for this experience, Francesca."

They spent an hour chatting and enjoying the cookies and tea. Josephine left her friend's house with the satisfaction of a renewed connection and Francesca's blessing over her choice in men.

Eighteen

Monday morning, while Cyrus's hired man painted Mathias's old room, Darla Adams arrived for her monthly herb purchase. Josephine brought her to the shed where they always chatted while she inspected the bundles and consulted her supply list. Though a midwife with several years' experience, Darla was only twenty and had married the previous spring.

"I know you haven't had your mother on this earth since childhood. Please understand I'm happy to help if you have any questions about things before your wedding."

Josephine looked into her kind, blue eyes. "Thank you, Darla. I might have questions, but not from what might happen because it already has."

Darla's broad face didn't register shock but her lips hinted at a knowing smile. "Go on, Jo."

"Is there a way to know which time—which joining is the one that creates a baby?"

"Are you concerned?"

"Not at all. The wedding is just over a week away, and we didn't have sex until this weekend."

"No one would be able to tell the difference in that short of a time, and there's no way of knowing the exact lovemaking experience if you're participating in the activity several times over a brief period. But there are only a few days a month you *can* get pregnant. The medical community as a whole hasn't accepted it, but there are some of us who follow what's considered folklore methods to prevent becoming pregnant."

She went on to explain the monthly cycle of a woman and counting days.

"But how do you keep your hands off him those days?"

Darla laughed. "There are other ways to please each other."

"Yes, we've been exploring things."

"I wish you well, Jo. And I'll happily come to you in your new location next month. Telephone if you ever need me."

Josephine thanked Darla and walked her to the front before going inside. She slipped the dollars from the sale into her coin purse and settled at her desk to go through the drawers. Her belongings needed to be packed in the coming days, and she spent the next hour productively.

At noon, Cyrus arrived to inspect the painting progress. After seeing all was well, he had dinner with Josephine in the dining room.

"As long as you're working here, I'll happily feed you, Mr. Harrington, even if Miss Jo isn't with you."

"Thank you, Miss Sarah. Would you consider coming to our house to work after the wedding? I know Jo appreciates your adaptive recipes."

With a tender gaze showing how touched she was, Sarah nodded and looked at Josephine. "I'd love to, but I couldn't leave without discussing it with Mr. Wolf and being sure he could find a replacement."

"Talk it over and let me know," Cyrus said.

Sarah nodded. "I will, Mr. Harrington. Thank you. I'm off to the market now, unless you need anything more."

"No thank you," Josephine replied. "We'll be fine."

Swirling a spoon through her soup, Josephine watched Cyrus while he buttered a slice of bread.

"Francesca telephoned this morning to thank us for visiting yesterday."

"She was delightful," Cyrus said with a smile.

"I'm sorry to say I've been neglecting her the past few months. She went through a depression when Tristan broke off their engagement, it wasn't much fun to sit in the bleak house with her and her invalid mother. I relied on Cordelia to keep her company since she's next door and her brother was the guilty party, but I should have been there more often."

"You're making amends now, Jo. That's what counts." Cyrus caressed her cheek. "But know you're everything to me, Jo, bringing me healing and love in abundance."

Josephine and Cyrus finished eating and moved upstairs. They were soon naked on her bed enjoying riotous pleasures. The old bed squeaked in protest against the onslaught of their rhythm. With her climax, Josephine clung to Cyrus in hopes he would follow. He did with a groan of submission.

Knocking tapped on the closed door.

"Josephine," Marlene called. "I was in the neighborhood and stopped by to check the progress. The kitchen door was unlocked, so I let myself in. Do you know when Mr. Harrington will be here?"

"Soon!" she called out as she rubbed against him.

"I'll wait for him in the parlor," Marlene called.

Redressed in a simple outfit she wore on gardening days, Josephine hastily braided her hair and pattered downstairs.

When Cyrus joined them, Marlene got right to business. "I looked in Mathias's old room when I first arrived and thought it much darker than we agreed upon."

"Paint turns lighter as it dries, Miss Jensen. I assure you that cornflower blue will be just what you're expecting by tomorrow. Coupled with the lighter wood tones of the new furniture, the room will be refreshingly crisp."

"I'm glad to hear that, Mr. Harrington. I do have ideas for Josephine's room since that will be open for a complete transformation as well. I want her room done over in pastels, the furniture sparse, so it could easily be changed over to a nursery if needed."

Cyrus settled on the sofa with his notebook. "How about yellow?"

"I can't abide yellow," Marlene said.

"What about sky blue? It would be lighter than the cornflower but complementary while still maintaining a cohesive palette."

"But wallpaper, like the first guest room, not paint."

Cyrus made a note. "I'll bring samples to you within the next few days."

"The bassinet and crib Mathias and I both used are in the attic, should they be needed," Josephine offered.

"Thank you, but my child will have no need for handed-down furniture. As far as I'm concerned, you may take whatever you want from this house that was here before the redecorating."

"Thank you." Josephine nearly choked on the words as Marlene played generous in giving away her parents' things.

Sensing Josephine's annoyance, Cyrus laid his hand on her knee and squeezed it lovingly. "What about the tones of the bay for the room's theme, Miss Jensen? And a few local artist's paintings to go with it."

"I like the sound of that, Mr. Harrington."

They chatted back and forth a few minutes more and he stood when she did.

"Shall I stay until Sarah returns?" Marlene asked.

"Since our engagement, my father has given Cyrus full access to the house. We don't need a chaperone."

She looked Josephine over. "Did you decide on the ceremony's location?"

Josephine nodded. "Magnolia Cemetery, at my mother's plot."

Revulsion marred Marlene's face.

"We don't want a large affair and it's close enough to make attending breakfast here afterward easy on the guests. I plan to write the invitations this afternoon. I'll include you and your parents, of course."

"How thoughtful of you, Josephine, though I'm not sure my parents' schedule will allow them to attend. But what will you wear, black?"

"I haven't decided on a dress yet."

"Do you need me to take you shopping?"

"No, thank you, Marlene."

"Well," she said and paused to switch to Cyrus's attention, "I look forward to seeing the wallpaper samples, Mr. Harrington."

Cyrus, needing to double-check the furniture delivery for the next day and hunt wallpaper, left not long after Marlene.

After sorting more items in her room, Josephine ventured to the attic to check what was in storage. The baby things, as she'd known, but also furniture pieces that looked promising including a rocking chair, fern stand, and dresser.

At supper, she asked her father about the items and told him what Marlene had said about taking what she wanted.

"I suppose there's nothing for me to hang onto if Marlene has her mind on something else."

"You have every right to keep your possessions, Papa. And don't let her orchestrate a remodel in your study. If you want it freshened, speak to Cyrus directly. You need to keep something of yourself when you marry her. I fear she'll change you completely."

"Jo, my girl." He patted her hand. "Thank you for caring. The fern stand was a wedding gift from an aunt. Your mother kept a flourishing Boston fern in it that withered without her care. I'm sure she'd love for you to put it to use."

After supper, father and daughter spent a quiet evening in the parlor, each reading their separate books.

In the morning, Josephine showed Cyrus around the attic. He agreed with her finds being great for their household and discovered several more items of interest, including her mother's wedding suit in an old trunk.

"The lace is gorgeous, Jo, and the aged tone would look wonderful against your complexion." Her mind began racing, but he continued. "I'll see if I can hire the delivery men to load this furniture and bring it to our house after they offload the new things."

"That's great, Cy. I'll be back in a bit." She gathered the clothing, kissed him goodbye, and dashed out the door.

Across Washington Square, Josephine pushed through the gate opposite the park and hurriedly knocked at the front of the house, setting Merritt's dog barking.

"Josephine, what in heaven's name is wrong?" Merritt Graves asked when she opened the door. "Velvet, stop that racket."

"Miss Merritt, I need your help." She shoved the wedding set at the petite woman. "I'm being married a week from tomorrow. I want to know if this could work for me."

Smiling, she balanced the clothing in one arm and put her other around Josephine to guide her inside. "I'd be happy to see what I could do, Josephine. It's beautifully preserved. Was it your mother's?"

She nodded.

"Let's go up to the guest room."

Josephine removed her outfit, pulled on the skirt, and buttoned the matching top which was typical of the previous century rather than the modern single piece gowns.

"It feels tight in my hips."

"And it's a little short. The train makes that obvious." Merritt circled Josephine, pursing her lips.

"So it's hopeless?"

Merritt inspected the fit of the shoulders and armpits, then down to the waist.

"Maybe not." She lifted the skirt and checked for excess fabric. "There's room on both seams to let things out, and if I cut the bottom two inches all the way around, I could redo the train into a wide trim. That is, if you'll allow me to try."

"Oh, yes, Merritt! Thank you!" She hugged her. "I'll give you all the herbs you want or cash or—"

She laughed. "Don't worry about that now. Let me get my measuring tape and write down the needed numbers. I'll send word when you can stop by for another fitting."

After the information was recorded, Josephine took off the ensemble. Merritt carefully laid it across the bed as a dark figure filled the doorway.

Merritt stifled a scream and Sean laughed.

"How dare you, Sean!" She rushed to the door. "You didn't even knock, did you?"

"I did at the kitchen door. No one answered, so I let myself in." His gaze raked over Josephine in her underclothes.

"You cad!" Merritt struck his stomach with a fist. "Josephine doesn't need you eyeing her like that!"

Sean grinned. "I've seen her similarly undressed before. Haven't I Jo?"

She showed him her middle finger and calmly buttoned the shirtwaist.

Merritt gasped and shoved him into the hall, closing the door behind them so Josephine could dress in private.

"Was that her wedding dress on the bed?" Sean's voice carried through the barrier.

"Yes, I'm fitting over her mother's set."

"I'm glad to hear that, Merri. Her fiancé appears to be a fine fellow."

With her black skirt refastened, Josephine opened the door. "What do you know of Cyrus?"

Sean smirked. "I know he impressed Alexander Melling when he purchased the St. Francis property. Alex tends to see through anyone because he used to be the biggest player in town. According to him, Cyrus Harrington's style and manners are impeccable. He's well educated, converses excellently, and manages to show all that without being arrogant."

Josephine lifted her chin defiantly. "It sounds like you could take some lessons from him."

Merritt laughed, and Sean poked her in the ribs.

"The house Mr. Harrington bought is only two blocks from my office. I'll have to stroll over on my lunch hours, Jo."

"Don't bother," she scolded.

"I haven't been in that house since late winter in '05. That was a hell of a poker game with Eliza and the boys."

"Why are you here?" Merritt asked as though trying to change the subject.

"I wanted to be sure you remembered my plea from Sunday evening. The one about being friendlier to Hattie the next time you see her."

"I'll not be told how to act within my own house, Sean."

"Yes, ma'am." He kissed her cheek and then turned towards Josephine.

"Don't even think about it."

"Oh, I can think about it, all right." He eyed her chest. "Thanks for allowing me to almost get a glimpse of those again." He winked before going downstairs.

"I'm sorry about that, Josephine," Merritt said with a sigh.

"It's not your fault Sean Spunner is the most arrogant man in Washington Square."

Merritt laughed. "He is, isn't he? I met his fiancée Saturday when they came to supper, and he doesn't think I was kind enough."

"How is she?"

"Shameless."

"So they're perfect for each other."

Merritt laughed. "I'll be sure to lock the door the next time we do a fitting. Thank you for thinking of me to do this for you. I'll give it my full attention."

***

That afternoon, Josephine visited Francesca alone.

Josephine leaned close where they sat together on the sofa. "You absolutely charmed Cyrus on Sunday."

Francesca's broad lips turned upwards in a smile. "He's the one who's charming. I don't believe I've ever seen a man as beautiful or eloquent as him. Thank you for introducing me. I don't want you to hide your joy because of what happened between me and Tristan."

"I'm glad you feel that way because I need your help." She squeezed Francesca's soft hands—the hands of a lady who played piano rather than weeded gardens. "I'm going shopping for a wedding gift for Cyrus, and I'd like your opinion. Would you go downtown with me tomorrow morning?"

"I'd like to but—"

"No excuses, Fran. I know there's a nurse here in the mornings to bathe your mother, but Merritt Graves is willing to come over as well to see that you get out of the house for a little while."

"Is Cordelia going too?" Francesca played with the tip of her dark braid that curved over her shoulder.

"She's busy on a new painting project and claims she can't be disturbed this week. But you and I can have a luncheon somewhere. And it's my treat. Papa gave me extra spending money to purchase what I need for the wedding and honeymoon trip."

"Do you need to go lingerie shopping?" Francesca whispered.

"A few new pieces wouldn't go amiss." Josephine grinned. "I'll be here at nine o'clock, all right?"

Francesca nodded. "Thank you, Jo."

"And I have an invitation for you, of course." She slipped the envelope out of her purse. "There's breakfast at our house immediately afterward, but I'll forgive you if you don't attend that. Cordelia's family could give you a ride. And no, Tristian isn't invited—just her and her parents."

Francesca hugged her friend, trying to hide her tears, but Josephine felt the tremor of emotions with the embrace.

Wednesday morning, Josephine stopped by George Street to collect Francesca. Francesca's rich brown hair was in a loose chignon worthy of a fashion magazine though her ensemble was from two winters ago.

"If we have time, I'd like to look at a few dresses for myself while we're out."

"Of course, Fran." Josephine squeezed her gloved hand. "It's a day of adventure for us. We haven't been to the city together in much too long."

After the streetcar ride into town, they began their search at Hammel's Department Store. While Francesca browsed, Josephine called to Mathias.

Good morning, Mat.

Hello, Jo.

Fran and I are in the woman's department. Do you have time to see us?

As soon as I finish this account I'm working on.

Wonderful. And please be extra nice to Fran. She's in need of cheering up.

A few minutes later, he arrived amid the ruffles and lace.

"Ah, my favorite sister!" Mathias kissed Josephine's cheek. "And Francesca! I haven't seen you in ages."

"Hello, Mathias." Francesca blushed as he took her hand and kissed her cheek as well. "I didn't expect you'd see us."

"And miss the chance to speak to Jo's cleverest friend? Never!" Mathias ran a hand across his smooth jaw and narrowed his arched brows, leaning in. "And I love any excuse to climb down from the accounting department. Do you need to open a line of credit today?"

Francesca laughed. "No, my father taught me to always pay with cash."

"Very smart, though keep the other option in mind for when you get a fancy for the season's newest bauble." He looked over her green dress. "You are lovelier than ever, but I do think a splash of blue would give you an even more attractive glow."

Mathias waved over a salesgirl, flirted with her a minute, then sent her off to find Francesca the perfect dress.

I forgot how much you love putting on a show. You should be an actor, Mat.

He flashed his debonair grin. *Francesca has always been a favorite, and as for the salesgirls—it's better if they think of me as another man chasing them.*

You love being adored.

I'm guilty as charged, Jo.

Mathias stayed long enough to applaud the blue dress when Francesca modeled it and managed to write off the delivery fee so Josephine and Francesca wouldn't need to wrestle with packages on the streetcar. Josephine said goodbye to Mathias, and then waited while Francesca added underclothes to her purchase before totaling it out.

While they were browsing the men's accessories, Josephine frowned. "It's all the same old things. Papa and Mat have been shopping here exclusively since Mat started his apprenticeship, but I want something different for Cyrus."

"My father always proclaimed Gayfer's the best choice, but there are specialty shops as well."

"We can try the other department store, then break for dinner," Josephine said. "And we'll walk by Cyrus's house so you can see where I'll be moving."

When Josephine and Francesca entered Gayfer's, the doorman pointed them in the direction of the men's department, promising to telephone ahead so their best clerk would be at their disposal when they arrived on the upper level.

The elevator doors opened and Edgar Melvin's smiling face immediately turned stony above his black suit.

Josephine lifted her chin defiantly. "I was informed the best would be waiting to help me."

"That's me, Witchy Wolf." Edgar crossed his arms. "What can I do for you?"

"Absolutely nothing." Josephine took Francesca's elbow and began roaming the display of neckties.

Edgar followed, cold eyes watching.

"We should leave, Jo," Francesca whispered. "I didn't realize he worked here."

"I'd like to finish walking the department so I can better compare the quality to other stores." Josephine fingered a silk handkerchief.

"Those come in sets of two," Edgar stated from behind them.

"I don't require information," Josephine said.

"It is policy for the salesclerks to assist customers, Witchy Wolf."

She turned on him, hazel eyes blazing. "And is it *policy*, Mr. Melvin, to harass the customers with taunting names?"

"It's customary to use the customer's name as often as possible to assure them we know and *care* about them, Witchy Wolf."

Josephine refused to meet his mocking grin and stalked toward the elevator, Francesca at her heels.

On the main floor, Josephine sought a manager.

"In all my shopping experiences, I have never felt so belittled," Josephine said in a rush of angst as soon as she was before the manager. "Edgar Melvin has no business assisting customers when he can't put his pettiness aside."

"I'm sorry, miss," the man stammered. "Mr. Melvin is typically one of our best men."

"Obviously his personal opinions are stronger than his ties to Gayfer's good name. I won't be back."

Blushing with embarrassment, Francesca followed Josephine outside. "He might get fired over that."

"I hope he is." Josephine looked toward Bienville Square and back to her friend. "Are you ready to eat?"

"How can you eat after that? I feel sick."

"Fran, listen to me." Josephine stood in front of her. "It was the most freeing thing to get that off my chest. I'm glad you steered us in there. Edgar has had it coming to him for a long time."

"But what will be coming to you in return?"

"There's nothing he can do to me that wouldn't end up with him in jail."

"Like Rupert Lyons?" Francesca whispered.

"I'd never take anything like what that woman went through. Come on, Fran. We won't let Edgar spoil our day."

They dined at the Vineyard Café, then strolled by Cyrus's house before trying a men's haberdashery on Dauphin Street. Josephine had handled Cyrus's hats often enough to have noticed the size. She picked out a dove gray fedora as well as pink handkerchiefs and a matching bowtie, all of which would do well for him on their wedding day.

By the time Josephine returned home, the incident with Edgar was long forgotten in favor of excitement over her gifts.

Cyrus arrived for supper not long after Mr. Wolf returned from work. Josephine gifted Cyrus his presents in the parlor, her father watching over them with a smile.

"Pink will be the color for us," Josephine said as Cyrus looked over the handkerchiefs. "It favors your coloring and is soft, like your touch. Would you make me a headpiece with pink roses for our wedding?"

"I'd be honored to, Jo." Cyrus kissed her lips. "Thank you. And I've been wanting to get a suit this color. The wedding is a wonderful excuse to do so."

Nineteen

Thursday, Josephine worked at transplanting herbs into terracotta pots all day in preparation for her move across town. Cyrus had a hired wagon collect what was ready that evening and transported them to his house.

On Friday, Josephine brought a change of clothes for taking supper out and arranged the transferred pots around the front porch at the St. Francis Street house while Cyrus was at work. He arrived home at noon with sandwiches from a delicatessen for a simple luncheon on the porch swing.

He motioned to the grouping of pots in the middle of the porch. "Are these the ones for the balcony?"

"Yes, they need more sun. I think they'll do well upstairs. I already have some others outside the kitchen steps."

"Have you been upstairs yet?"

Josephine shook her head.

"Then allow me to help before I have to leave."

They went upstairs, each carrying a potted plant.

The bedroom, previously bare of decorations, sported several new items including pale blue-gray walls. On the long wall across from the hall door, the center section between the French doors to the balcony had a watercolor of Washington Square. It complemented Josephine's birthday present from Cordelia that hung over the fireplace with a gorgeous matte and scrolling frame.

"I commissioned her," Cyrus said. "Fortunately, Cordelia works quickly. And look!"

He nodded to the left side of the room. The side wall beyond the brass bed featured a painting of a camellia bush in bloom. And above the bed, a watercolor of a magnolia tree in May.

"I wanted to be sure you were surrounded by lush beauty. As soon as I'm established, I'll move you out of the city, Jo."

"Wherever you are is home, Cy, but all this is gorgeous."

"I'm pleased you like it." He set down the pot, then took hers as well so he could embrace her. "I love you, Jo."

The remainder of the plants were soon relocated to the upper balcony, Cyrus carrying the rest so Josephine could arrange them as she wished. By the time Cyrus returned to work, Cordelia had been telephoned and was on her way over.

An hour later, Josephine was on her knees on the east side of the house, adding nutrients to the barren soil and turning it with a hand spade in preparation for transplanting several shrubs from her father's house that Midnight enjoyed prowling around.

Cordelia was perched on an upside-down milk crate. "Did you know Cyrus commissioned me for more watercolors? Two paintings of Mobile Bay will soon be hanging in your old room."

"That's wonderful. I love the ones you did for our bedroom."

"How is Mathias doing?"

Josephine shrugged. "All right, I suppose. He has a masquerade to attend tonight for the society he pledged to this year. I hope he doesn't do anything asinine."

"Tonight? Don't tell me he's going with Mystics of Dardenne!"

"Then I won't tell you."

"I wish I could go. It's said there's no better show of debauchery. If I can't live it, I might as well observe it."

"Del, you're an intelligent and talented woman, but when you talk like that, *you* sound asinine. If romance is meant to happen for you, it will."

"I'm destined for the convent and you know it. I only wish painting could be my life-long vocation. I'd be happy if I could paint and live a life of freedom with my friends around me."

Hands too dirty for hugging, Josephine kissed Cordelia's cheek. "If Cyrus commissions you for every house he does, would that be enough to live on?"

"Possibly, but he has to keep his own commissions going after he finishes Marlene's rooms. Besides, he might be too busy with the tableaus and floats to focus much on interior design."

"I'm certain of his success, whichever platforms he uses, as well as people recognizing your talent."

"I never expected you to be the sappy sort, Jo, but you're smitten with him. At least it's for good reason." Cordelia stood. "I should leave if I'm going to capture a sketch of Bienville Square before I meet my parents for supper at the Trellis Room."

"Enjoy your time, Del. Stop in again. Cyrus works tomorrow morning, but I'll be here if you want to come back then."

"I'd love to."

Soon after Cordelia left, Josephine washed off the day's toil in preparation for the evening, but stayed in fresh underclothes rather than put on the gown she'd brought with her that morning. She tied on Cyrus's robe and relaxed on the sofa in the front room.

When Cyrus arrived, he dropped to a knee beside her. "I love coming home to you. Wednesday can't come soon enough, Jo."

They retreated to the bedroom. His gorgeous blue eyes, stroking hands, and undying rhythm permeated her senses until they dressed for supper at the Cawthon Hotel.

***

First thing Saturday morning, Mr. Wolf brought Josephine, Cordelia, and several bushes dug up from their yard to Cyrus's house. Before leaving for work, Cyrus made sure Josephine had everything she needed to transplant the azaleas.

When finished with the bushes, Josephine and Cordelia settled on the porch swing, discussing the possibility of Cordelia using twigs and leaves to paint some experimental designs.

Jo, can you hear me? A weak voice said.

Mat? What's wrong? She jerked upright, senses heightened.

"Jo? Are you okay?" Cordelia asked.

She shook her head and strained to hear her brother. Something was seriously wrong with him. *Mat, try again. I lost you.*

Jo...

I'm here. If you can't focus enough to speak, stay quiet. I'll find you. I promise.

Josephine closed her eyes, slumped against the swing, and concentrated on Mathias. Her spiritual senses stretched beyond the porch like wings as she imagined the building his apartment was in. Her spirit rose toward the clouds. Flying to Dauphin Street, she peered inside the windows of his second-floor rooms.

Empty.

Temperance Hall, the scene of last night's masquerade was her next stop. All the windows and doors were closed. Then the back door of the building burst open and a handful of Mystics of Dardenne members partially disrobed from their devil costumes stumbled into the alley, oblivious to a spirit hovering above them.

"Do you think he'll come to before the cleaning team arrives?" one asked.

Edgar pulled his facemask off and smirked. "He can never wake up for all I care. That beating is what Wolf gets for being too proud of his pretty face."

"He needed to be taken down a notch, the arrogant greenie," another added.

Edgar nodded and rubbed his reddened knuckles. "His face is no longer perfect."

Rowdy laughter followed them as the men sang a bawdy tune on their way toward the red-light district.

It took all Josephine's control to return peacefully to her body. When she settled back on the porch swing, she took a gasping breath.

"What happened?" Cordelia asked.

"I had to find Mat. He's in bad shape, Del. I need help."

"Cyrus is a telephone call away."

"Cyrus doesn't understand the way these bachelor societies work, and he's not keen on Mathias's behavior." Josephine paced the porch. "Sean! He knows exactly what goes on there. I once followed him to a Dardenne masquerade."

"And you never told me about it?"

"Now isn't the time, Del." Josephine plopped back onto the swing. "I need a minute."

Sean Spunner, I know you can hear me. I desperately need your assistance. I need you to meet me at Temperance Hall to help collect Mathias. I expect you can reach there from anywhere in the city within a half hour, but if you happen to be out of town, telephone me within the next few minutes to let me know.

Josephine jumped to her feet and turned to Cordelia. "I need you to listen out for the telephone while I get ready."

Shoes and jacket donned, Josephine bid goodbye to Cordelia, hurried down the porch steps, and headed up the next block.

The three-story building looked as it had minutes before from her astral view. Even if Edgar and his friends were gone, she had no way of knowing if anyone was inside beside Mathias.

She let herself in the back door and paused to allow her eyes to adjust to the dimness before making her way to the main room. The wooden floor echoed her steps in the cavernous space that often served as a roller-skating rink and the arena for boxing tournaments. A few people were passed out along the walls, masks off. None were Mathias.

From what she witnessed while shadowing Sean Spunner in January of 1904, Josephine knew the society members who rented the building utilized private rooms on the upper floors to participate in activities they didn't want the general guests to be privy to. She climbed the stairs as lightly as possible through the eerie quiet.

On the second floor, she heard the murmur of voices from an open room.

"I hear something," a voice said as she approached.

"Go look."

Shuffling steps.

A moment later, a young man partially disrobed from his Mystics of Dardenne costume startled.

"It's a lady," he said over his shoulder.

"The whores are back?"

"No," he said slowly. "A real lady. I think I've seen her around town before, but I can't remember."

"You couldn't remember your own name right now if it wasn't sewn into your underdrawers." The man laughed as he joined the other in the doorway. "Fellas, we got ourselves a little lady who needs to be shown a good time."

"Don't even think about it," Josephine said with deadly calm. "I'm here to get my brother. If any of you remember how to be a gentleman, I'll gladly accept your assistance locating him."

The laughing man swaggered toward her unsteadily. "I'd rather show you what I could do for you in private."

"Touch me and my lawyer will sue you for every pathetic thing you own."

He snorted. "No one can get charges to stick during Mardi Gras."

"Solicitor Spunner could." Sean's name rolled off her tongue easier than she liked.

"As if we believe that you have him in your pocket."

"Never doubt the word of a lady, my friends." Sean's voice carried from the stairwell. He strolled down the hall with bravado, his fiancée on his arm as if they were taking an afternoon walk in the park.

The man gaped, then waved his hand in dismissal. "Go on."

Josephine went for the next flight of stairs, Sean and Hattie following. On the third floor, Sean took Josephine's elbow with his free hand.

"Thank you for coming, Sean."

"Do you wish to wait here while I look for him?" Sean asked.

"No, I can handle it."

He looked at his fiancée.

"Don't try to shield me, Sean," Hattie replied.

"Fair enough, ladies. Welcome to my old stomping grounds."

Grunts, moans, and the smell of sex, alcohol, and blood crept around them like tentacles forcing them into the vile domain.

I'm here, Mat. I just need another minute to find you.

"The member den is this one." Sean motioned into a shadowed space where the undesirable sounds were coming from. A quick look inside showed many of the fainting couches around the room populated by couples actively working towards climax or passed out from the aftereffects of it.

Jo…

She shifted back into the hall. "Are there no private rooms?"

Sean motioned to the handful of doors further on. "But you can't barge into those, darling."

"I have to find Mathias."

"Start with the furthest one. If something bad was going on, they'd want it far away to keep it from being discovered." Sean dropped Hattie's arm and hurried ahead with Josephine.

He reached for the knob first. The light from the hall rushed into the darkness with the spreading rectangle of brightness across the bare floor save for Sean's shadow. Mathias lay on the wood boards, swollen face barely recognizable and bleeding as he was curled on his side, making himself as small as possible.

"Mat, I'm here." Josephine said as she knelt beside him. "I'll get you home."

His split lips parted and he heaved for breath.

"Try to stay calm, Mat." Josephine looked up at Sean. He nodded, squatted down, and hefted Mathias to his feet.

"I can't carry him all the way," Sean said. "We'll have to hold him between us."

They put Mathias's arms around their shoulders and walked together for the stairs. The steps were tricky, but they managed to stay upright, Hattie spotting them from the front. Mathias fainted for a brief time, but Josephine was glad he was out of pain for the moment. On the ground floor, Sean motioned toward the back hall. Hattie held the door for them to exit. The sun momentarily blinded Josephine before the respite of Sean's automobile came into view.

Hattie opened the rear passenger door and Sean heaved Mathias onto the bench.

"To the hospital?" Sean asked.

No hospital, no police.

You need to press charges, Mat! What Edgar did to you was unjustified.

He did it in retaliation of you ratting him out at Gayfer's.

Heart sinking, Josephine gently touched his hand. *He needs to stop taking his frustration with me out on you. You must tell what happened, Mat.*

No Mystics of Dardenne brother rats another out.

And no true brother would do such a thing!

"He refuses the hospital," Josephine told Sean. "Bring him to my house and I'll telephone Darla Adams."

Sean parked in the back, and Cordelia held the kitchen door open. She looked like looming death in her typical black ensemble with a concerned face to match. Sean carried Mathias the short distance into the house. Catching Cordelia's eye, Josephine instructed her to lead the way to the only guest room with a bed. Hattie followed them.

Josephine stopped in the kitchen long enough to telephone Darla, begging her to come with medical supplies.

Upstairs, Cordelia was crying and Mathias groaning while Sean and Hattie looked on from the corner of the room.

"Del, please watch for Darla Adams to arrive."

"The midwife?"

"She's an experienced medical professional. If she can't help, she'll know who can. And boil some water, just in case."

She looked once more at Mathias before retreating with a choking sob.

"Will you hold him up while I remove his shirt?" Josephine asked Sean. "And, Hattie, could you go to the bathroom and bring a damp cloth for his head?"

Hattie left the room and Sean held Mathias upright while Josephine carefully removed the shirt, as well as his socks and shoes. Once he was arranged on the bed, she covered Mathias with a cotton blanket from the linen closet and gently placed the cold cloth on his forehead.

"Beside the face strikes, it looks like kidney punches and booted kicks once he was down, but he has defensive wounds on his hands. He went down fighting, though I bet he was outnumbered five to one." Sean shook his head. "Does he wish to name the assailants and press charges?"

"Unfortunately not. He claims some Mystics of Dardenne code of ethics forbids it, though apparently it doesn't frown on assaulting each other."

Sean shrugged. "Every few years there's a shift in the group. The worst thing that happened between members in my day was one guy punching another over his attempt to handle his fiancée. Let me know if he changes his mind, though I doubt he will. I should thank you for the trip down memory lane. After witnessing the horrid aftermath of the masquerade, I'm more pleased than ever to be out of these ranks."

"It was an education," Hattie said.

"Hattie, dearest, you need an introduction." Sean took her hand. "I'd like to officially introduce you to Jo Wolf, soon to be Josephine Harrington. And yes, she's as feisty as her name. Jo, this is Hattie Fernsby, my fiancée."

"Hello, Hattie. I must confess, I'm not sure if I should congratulate you or commiserate your choice."

"I suppose that does vary by the hour with Sean." Hattie's bright smile shone all the way to her merry blue eyes.

Josephine grinned at the thought that the woman might actually be able to handle him.

Sean caught her smirk and returned it as he crossed his arms. "I told you that you'd like her, Jo."

She lifted an eyebrow. "I appreciate your service, Sean, and you accompanying him, Hattie. I couldn't have gotten him here without you."

Darla arrived a few minutes later. "Your brother's injuries could be beyond me, Josephine. I'll examine him and help you clean him, but he might have to go to the hospital." She rolled up her sleeves and opened her bag. "I need sterile water, clean cloths, and towels."

Josephine spent the next half hour being an assistant to Darla while Cordelia, Sean, and Hattie waited in the hallway.

As terrible as Mathias looked, his wounds appeared to be surface damage only, except for a concussion and a few damaged ribs. Once he was washed, Darla wrapped Mathias's chest to bind the bruised and broken ribs. He only whimpered off and on throughout the ordeal, but Josephine knew he was alert.

"Shall I have Dr. Hughes send in a prescription for pain medicine, or would you prefer to use whiskey?"

"Whiskey, to keep the involvement down to as few people as possible."

Darla nodded and pushed a loose strand of hair off her forehead with the back of her hand.

"I can't thank you enough, Darla. Go over your time and efforts and send me the bill. I'll pay it straight away."

"I appreciate it, Jo. And to think I almost went to medical school last year. I'm getting plenty of hands-on training without it."

When they opened the door, Josephine let the others know Mathias would be all right.

"Will you watch him while I see Darla down?" she asked Cordelia.

"Of course."

"And Sean, could you buy a bottle of whiskey? Cyrus doesn't keep anything hard in the house, but we need it for medicinal use."

"I'd be happy to help, darling."

Sean offered to give Darla a ride home and left with her and Hattie. When Josephine returned upstairs, Cordelia was perched on a dining chair beside the guest bed.

You have an angel at your side, Mat.

Two of them.

I'm more devil than angel and you know it. If I hadn't set things off with Edgar at Gayfer's, none of this—

He would have found an excuse eventually, Jo.

I'll figure out a way to stop him.

Sean and Hattie returned with the whiskey. Josephine declined any more help and thanked them for all they had done. Ignoring Sean's arrogant smirk, she embraced him.

You were right about Hattie, Sean. She's perfect for you—fiery and bold like your favorite color, Josephine told him. *I wish you the best.*

She hugged Hattie as well. "It was wonderful to meet you, though I'm sorry for the circumstance. I wish you all the happiness in the world, Hattie."

"Thank you. I'm sure your brother will heal quickly. I've never seen such efficiency in a medical professional so young before. Darla is amazing."

Josephine agreed and saw them to the door.

Not long after they left, Cyrus returned home and found Josephine ruminating on the sofa.

"What's wrong, Jo?"

As soon as he sat beside her, she fell into Cyrus's arms in an attempt to ease the pain she felt she'd caused her brother.

"Mathias is upstairs. He looks nearly dead, but Darla said the worst is a concussion and broken ribs. He was beaten by Edgar and his friends this morning at the masquerade."

Cyrus passed her a handkerchief from his breast pocket.

"I won't ask you to help care for him, but I would like him to stay here until he's mended enough to look after himself."

"Of course, Jo. He's your brother."

"Thank you. Cordelia is sitting with him right now, and Darla is supposed to stop in tomorrow to check on him."

"The midwife you sell herbs to?"

"Yes, but she's so much more. Would you be willing to go to his apartment and collect clothes for him, as well as the canister of my healing tea blend from Papa's house? Miss Sarah knows which one it is."

"Certainly. And I'll pick up deli sandwiches on the way back."

Before long, Mathias slept in his own nightshirt under the effects of the whiskey and the others dined together.

At Cyrus's insistence, Josephine rested on the chaise lounge in their bedroom. After his loving attention, several minutes alone helped her absorb a bit of peace—the first she'd had since sitting with Cordelia in the swing that morning. She reached over and set the revolving bookcase on a slow spin. It now housed a few dozen of her books. When it stopped, the stack she'd acquired from Mrs. Rettig faced her. Josephine fingered the worn spines, wondering how she could squash Edgar's bullying once and for all.

Knowing she must find the man and expose more of her abilities than she wished to protect her brother, Josephine's spirit flew west without hesitation. The Creole neighborhood formed one of the invisible borders of the red-light district, probably because the men who frequented it knew their wives would never venture too close. The soft, mournful sound of a solitary trumpet came from the Creole fire station.

Josephine circled the few blocks that housed the working girls. It had been years since she'd spied on the happenings in the bordellos, but the chance of finding Edgar Melvin gave an edge of excitement to the sleuthing.

Josephine began at the swankiest house. It boasted an opulent Victorian parlor complete with red velvet draperies, crystal chandeliers, and scrolling rosewood furniture pieces. Since it was in the middle of the afternoon, there were only a couple women in the common room showering a mature guest with attentions in hopes of winning their pay for the evening while the madam watched over them, hand on the decanter.

Upstairs were a few balding men—the ones who could afford the luxuries the top house offered—being serviced by the prettiest painted ladies in Mobile.

Four locations later, she found the flaming head of Edgar. He was dressed in a simple suit and sat in a private parlor that had seen better days but kept its air of refinement as though to remind the visitors the house offered a touch of something more. He was flipping through a scrapbook. The house matron sat beside him in a low-cut evening gown.

Josephine perched on the arm of the settee and looked over his shoulder at the photograph on the page. The woman depicted had a crop in her hand and a mischievous smile on her painted lips.

"Do you wish another session with Rosaleigh?" the woman asked. "She's a favorite for a reason."

"She's too soft. I need more," Edgar said as he turned the page. He pointed to the woman depicted, who held a paddle and smirked. "She was a joke."

"Well," the madam said, "if you are willing to pay more, there is something else I could offer. That is, if you are serious and these girls no longer offer you enough pain and pleasure."

"Yes, I'll pay whatever, so long as I get the proper punishment."

Josephine's eyes widened over the eagerness in his voice.

The woman slowly moved across the room, the rustle of silk hypnotic with the sway of her hips. She retrieved a key from her bosom and unlocked a drawer in the dainty secretary hutch. With a smile, she returned with a ledger and portrait. She passed the glossy photograph of a man and woman wearing scant togas, full face gladiator helmets, and wielding a short sword and spear respectively. The poses they held between the Roman columns in their short, sleeveless tunics showcased their strength while the battle helmets hid their identities.

"Maximus and Domitia might be what you're looking for. This is their hobby, and the limited time they apply to these appointments are part of what you're paying for, but I assure you they know exactly what they're doing. You get them both or neither. The price is for two hours. They are allowed to do anything they want to you—the both of them."

Edgar licked his lips and looked from the picture to the woman.

"Yes," she whispered. "You understand. Many patrons find this is what they were looking for when a single female isn't enough to punish what they think they need to repent of in their deepest thoughts."

"Is that Frederick Davenport?" Edgar fingered the outline of Maximus's broad chest and biceps.

"The reigning heavyweight champion of Mobile, no." The madam smiled, and Josephine nodded in agreement that the man's form was as fine as the local boxer's who had chipped Sean's tooth all those years ago. "But I can assure you he is just as fit and handsome, though you will never see his face. His body, I'm sure you can see, will more than make up for that. And Domitia is strength and beauty combined. They are a glorious team that will bring you to your knees."

"I'll take them."

Madame opened her book. "They will be here a week from Saturday and have an appointment available. The full deposit must be made the day before. You cannot change your mind once your appointment is paid for."

"Yes, yes. I'll do it."

"Then I expect you to deliver twenty dollars to me by Friday, January seventeenth. I'm sure you'll agree that it's money well-spent, Mr. Melvin."

He blanched at the amount, but nodded.

Josephine flew to the sky in glee, circling the house as the sun set to expel the delight she had in knowing that she had enough to quell Edgar.

When he exited the house a few minutes later, Josephine floated inches behind him. With a quick flick of her wrist, she sent his fedora skidding down the sidewalk. Edgar grumbled, paused to pick it up, and then continued.

It's a minor annoyance, isn't it Edgar? That's what you've been to me all these years.

Edgar stopped and looked around at the growing shadows.

You've been crossing lines since you were a child, but this morning you stepped over one that cannot be ignored.

He paled as his eyes swept the empty street. "How…" he started to say, but then dashed south.

Josephine stayed with him. *You cannot outrun me, Edgar Melvin! I am after all a witch, as you like to remind me and everyone around you. Stop at the next corner so you can be sure to concentrate on what I'm about to tell you.*

Edgar plowed across Dauphin Street. Josephine kept by his shoulder and screeched like a banshee. He tripped, stumbling to the ground. Trembling, he rose to his feet, eyes wide as he searched his surroundings for the disembodied voice.

I suggest you stay where you are. Josephine leaned close enough to see the sweat beading his brow. *If you ever hurt my brother again you may be sure that your paid punishments in the red-light district will look like silly games compared to the torment I'll put you through. Poison, broken bones, and even lawsuits will be in your future if you ever harass or harm Mathias again. Do you understand?*

Edgar nodded.

I want to hear you say the words, Edgar.

"I won't touch him."

Or send anyone else to, or badmouth, or even think about it.

"No, never!" Edgar crossed his arms to hide their shaking.

Good, because I'll know. Now say my name and promise me.

"I promise, Wit—Josephine Wolf—not to bother or hurt Mathias."

You've been warned, Edgar. Now go home.

Josephine rose thirty feet above the road to watch until his running form was to Government Street before turning back to Cyrus's house with a pleased grin.

Twenty

"Are you sure she's all right, Cordelia?" Cyrus asked.

"I'd bet my life she's in one of her spirit trances," Cordelia replied.

Cyrus's warm hand was on her cheek. "Jo, my love, are you well?"

Josephine opened her eyes and smiled. "Quite well. And yes, Del was correct."

"Warn him next time," Cordelia said. "He's never been on this end of it before."

"I'm sorry, Cy." Josephine's arms went around his shoulders. "There was something I had to do."

"Taking care of Edgar, I hope." Cordelia's tone was harsh.

She nodded. "Mathias will be safe from now on—we all will."

They gathered in the guest room and Josephine shared her story of what she had witnessed and done to Edgar. Cordelia was amused, but Mathias was silent except for whimpers and moans when forced to move in order to take a few sips of Josephine's healing tea blend.

Cordelia's father picked her up at seven, though she was reluctant to leave. Josephine promised she would be welcomed the next day.

After supper, Josephine visited the guest room while Cyrus showered.

"Do you want me to stay in here with you tonight, Mat?"

He tried to open his eyes, but they were mere slits amid the purple swelling.

No, go home or be with Cyrus.

"Call to me if you need anything."

I will. And thank you. I still can't believe what you did to Edgar. You are *a witch—or something that rhymes with it, Jo. And I approve.*

She took his hand, keeping away from his bandaged knuckles. "I'll always be here for you, Mat."

After a telephone call to her father to explain that she wouldn't be home because she was helping Mathias heal from an altercation, Josephine stripped to her underclothes. She spent the night spooned with Cyrus and woke rested before six in the morning.

As though waiting to feel her alertness, Mathias called out. *Jo, could you help me?*

I'll be right there. Josephine silently slipped out of Cyrus's arms and dressed.

At her brother's bedside, she assisted him to a sitting position and then standing. Mathias winced and cursed several times as she walked him to the bathroom.

While waiting outside the door, Cyrus exited his bedroom, tying a blue robe over his nakedness. "I'll start the water for coffee."

"Thank you. I'll be down as soon as I can."

There was a moan from the closed bathroom.

"Shall I come in, Mat?"

Yeah, I'm covered. It hurts to talk because my face looks like raw meat. No wonder you don't eat it. It's disgusting.

He was leaning against the pedestal sink for support.

"Let's get you back to bed. Do you wish breakfast?"

It hurts too much to think about chewing. Let me have another shot of whiskey and then maybe I'll take some broth midday.

He drank before he lay down, and Josephine gently covered him.

Once he was settled, she pattered down the stairs to the kitchen, following the aroma of freshly ground coffee beans.

"Have I ever told you how much I adore your freckles?" Cyrus lightly kissed the tip of Josephine's nose.

"Once, during our first time together."

"Good, because I do." Cyrus caught her secret smile and kissed the corner of her mouth. "I love that curling grin too."

"Are you going to show me how much you do?" she teased.

"I think I hear knocking."

She followed Cyrus to the front.

"I hope I'm not too early," Cordelia said when he opened the door.

"We've been up for a while but excuse my attire." Cyrus motioned her inside.

Cordelia lifted a paper bag. "I brought pastries, if that is any consolation to my earliness."

"Thank you, Cordelia. I was just preparing the coffee. Allow me to dress, then I'll finish that for us." Cyrus kissed Josephine's cheek before going upstairs.

Cordelia set aside the bag and removed her coat. "How's the patient?" she asked Josephine.

"Mathias was up to use the bathroom about six, and then took a shot of whiskey. He'll probably sleep a while longer, but I'll go check him."

When she returned to the kitchen, Cyrus and Cordelia were at the table, talking like conspirators.

"Do I want to know what's being discussed?"

"Great plans for incorporating Cordelia's art into my projects." Cyrus poured Josephine coffee from the carafe. "Our bedroom is all the better for her paintings."

"So it is," she agreed.

"The jar," Cordelia pointed to a lidded pint glass next to the pastries. "My mom's cinnamon applesauce for you, Jo."

"Thank you!"

"She has more, but I couldn't manage it all this morning."

"Don't worry about that now. This is perfect for my breakfast. I think it would be good for Mat too. He told me he didn't want to eat anything, but would try to drink some broth later."

Cordelia sighed. "I wish I could take the pain from him."

After they were done in the kitchen, Cordelia brought her sketchbook to the guest room to watch over Mathias, where she spent several hours while he was asleep and awake.

Midafternoon, Josephine delivered a dish of applesauce.

Cordelia leaned forward to take it. "I'll help you, Mat."

"It's small enough for me to hold," he mumbled, barely opening his mouth to say it.

They looked at him in surprise.

"I can talk, I just choose not to because it hurts."

"Why don't you take a walk around the block, Del?" Josephine suggested. "We don't want you languishing while you're by the sick bed."

"If you think you'll be fine without me."

"We'll manage." She shifted toward the hall to give Cordelia a path out of the room.

"Go, Del," Mathias said.

She frowned and stood.

Mathias grabbed her hand. "I didn't mean it like that. I appreciate your time and efforts to entertain me. I've grown fond of you and your stubby nose."

Cordelia laughed.

"It's much prettier than mine at the moment."

"You have a lovely nose—and ears, lips, and eyes."

"Not right now."

"It's still there beneath the swelling. I see the real you, not the monster you think you are."

Mathias hissed. "Don't make me smile. That's the worst."

"Then allow me to make you smile when you've healed. I'd enjoy being friends with you."

"Do me a favor and show up in something besides black tomorrow. It's dreary enough being stuck in bed without looking at a Gothic nun all day."

"So long as you pose nude for me at least once."

Mathias choked on a laugh, grabbing for his ribs. "Go, Del. Leave me to the applesauce so I needn't smile."

Mathias stayed at Cyrus's house another day. Monday evening, Cordelia—dressed in red—escorted Mathias down the stairs so he could practice sitting at a table with his bound ribs since he would have to do that for work, not to mention the wedding Wednesday morning. Josephine took the seat Cyrus pulled out for her and watched her brother and best friend arrive.

Cordelia pulled out Mathias's chair and patted his shoulder beneath his puffy, discolored face. "You did well, Mat. I'm proud of you."

"And I love you like a stray puppy that followed me home, but I'm a cat person."

She turned away, playfully pouting.

"Del, don't be like that. You're adorable and exasperating and devoted. I appreciate that you've been so giving to me these past days, including wearing cheerful colors for my benefit. If I ever get my face back to normal, you'd be a wonderful ornament on my arm when necessary. We might do well in keeping each other out of trouble—and the convent— but I could never give you more than a platonic friendship."

"I understand, Mat. I have for a long time. You never eyed girls like my brothers did growing up. Devoting myself to being your bosom friend and my painting pursuits would be a much truer life than I ever could have with a pious existence."

Mathias nodded, the hint of a smirk playing on his split lips. "It's too dangerous for you to join a convent. You might be ravished by a priest."

Cordelia's eyes widened. "That's a possibility I hadn't thought of! What's the penalty of reconsidering, Mat?"

He grinned, arm around his ribs as though reminding himself not to laugh. "Do you have your eye on Father De Fiore too?" They shared a secretive smile. "You know we're a good team when we're attracted to the same men. What's your opinion on Mr. Spunner?"

"I may have tried to offer myself to him when he was apologizing to Jo."

"Ha! I only wish I hadn't been delirious with pain when he helped Jo take off my shirt the other day. The fantasy would have been exquisite. But Jo, I think I'm well enough to go home tonight," Mathias said over his soup bowl.

"I could go with you," Cordelia offered.

"And get a reputation by going into a bachelor's apartment?" he asked.

"I've always wanted a reputation," she admitted.

Mathias chuckled. "I think you're going to be more of a handful than me."

Twenty-one

Wednesday morning at seven-thirty, Josephine stood in her room before the dressing table mirror in her mother's made over wedding suit. Sarah brought up a circlet of fresh pink roses and placed it on Josephine's head.

"Cyrus sent his love when he delivered it," Sarah said. "And he says there is a surprise for you at the cemetery. You're beautiful, Miss Jo."

"Call me Jo from now on. There's no need for formalities." She hugged her.

"It's been a pleasure to watch you grow up. I look forward to starting work at your new home next week."

"Sarah, the Barnes family is here to take you to the ceremony!" Mr. Wolf called upstairs.

She fluffed Josephine's sleeves and patted her chignon that was topped with the roses, making sure it was secure. "I'll see you soon."

Josephine followed Sarah downstairs, grinning at her father.

"You're as pretty as your mother, Josephine. I know she'd be touched by you honoring her today. Are you ready?"

She nodded, and he escorted her to the horse-drawn carriage gleaming black in the morning sun. The *clip-clop* of the horses' hooves reminded Josephine of childhood rides about town. As promised, the coachman drove around the north side of Washington Square so Josephine could wave at Merritt Graves, who waited at her gate.

The only clergyman Mr. Wolf could find willing to marry a couple in a cemetery who was not of the same faith was a young Protestant minister who insisted on two dollars and a bottle of wine for payment. He stood regally enough in his black vestments before Helen Wolf's angel monument, but Josephine's eyes were on the man in the dove gray suit.

Cyrus James Harrington, the keeper of her soul. His side part was as precise as ever, his pink bowtie and triangle of the matching handkerchief in his breast pocket immaculate. His beaming smile shone on her as Mr. Wolf handed Josephine out of the carriage.

Standing in an arch framing the plot—Josephine thought chairs unnecessary for the short ceremony—were Francesca, Cordelia, Mr. and Mrs. Barnes, Sarah, Marlene, Mathias (sporting his colorful bruising), and a woman who could only be Cyrus's mother. Mrs. Harrington's corseted figure was wrapped in a gray House of Worth traveling suit.

Mr. Wolf placed Josephine's hand into Cyrus's and stepped back to stand by Marlene.

Seeing the minister's bloodshot eyes up close, Josephine feared over his promised short nuptials, but he kept to the task. No rambling sermon about obeying the husband, only their promises and joining them before God.

A few minutes later, Cyrus and Josephine slipped matching gold bands onto each other's ring fingers as a murder of crows flew overhead before roosting in a nearby cedar tree.

The couple kissed while Cordelia clapped. Dressed in her typical black, she was the first to greet them after they separated.

"This was the most romantic wedding ever! I'll see you soon, but we have to get Francesca and Miss Sarah home."

Josephine hugged Cordelia and then Francesca, thanking them both for coming. The five left in Mr. Barnes's automobile, and the minister settled beneath the cedar tree with his bottle of wine.

Mr. Wolf and Marlene were already introducing themselves to Mrs. Harrington, but joined Mathias at their automobile when Cyrus approached his mother with Josephine.

"Mother, may I introduce you to—"

Her dainty, gloved hands cupped Josephine's face. "Dear Josephine, the woman my Cyrus loves more than anything. You're already my favorite daughter-in-law. I brought you a gift to thank you for your heart-felt letter." Reaching into the pocket of her suit jacket, she pulled out a silver strand sparkling with blue. "My husband refuses to acknowledge Cyrus, but I'll not be stopped, especially when I know he's living an honest life with the one he loves. These were my mother's, but they're yours now, Josephine. Welcome to the family. I'm sorry I can't stay more than a few minutes more, but I must catch the next train back to Atlanta."

Josephine clasped the jewels. "Surely you could stay the night, Mrs. Harrington. We'd gladly put off our trip to have a day with you."

"You're too kind, my dear, but you don't know my husband. I'm in enough trouble for coming, but I had to see for myself that I was right." Holding her hand, she went to Cyrus and took one of his with her other. Her blue eyes were as soft as a kitten's as she looked from Josephine to her son. "Your father tried to tell me your letter was a ruse to get in our good graces, but I knew you weren't capable of such trickery. My Cyrus has a pure heart. You were never like your brothers and that always pleased me. Your grandmamma would have adored Josephine. She's just the type for you, dearest. I know you'll treat her well."

Openly crying, Cyrus embraced his mother. They held each other while Josephine silently witnessed the tender scene.

"Cyrus, I must get back to the station." She kissed his cheek.

"Visit us soon. I'll fix a guest room for you with every comfort, Mother."

"It would be a pleasure to host you," Josephine agreed.

"Write to me often. I'll return as soon as I can."

Cyrus escorted his mother to the waiting automobile. When the black car pulled away, Cyrus stared after it for several moments. Then he lifted his wife off the lawn with a hug so huge she nearly disappeared into him.

"She came! She came and she loves you!"

"She loves *you*, Cyrus."

"To think she brought Grandmamma's necklace in her pocket. Where is it?"

Josephine opened her hand.

"It's white gold and sapphires, a one-of-a-kind piece made by a jeweler in Savannah, where Grandmamma was from." Cyrus stood behind Josephine. He kissed her neck with a lingering quality before stringing the necklace around her throat. The triad of sapphire pendants rested on the swell of her chest. "You make it glow, my gorgeous bride."

"It's my turn for introductions." Josephine took Cyrus back to the headstone. "Mama, Cyrus will take diligent care of me. I know you would love him almost as much as I do. I'll be living on the north side of town, so I won't get over here as often, but I'll be thinking of you."

Stepping out of the carriage in front of the Wolfs' house, they were approached by a photographer.

"Stay for a moment, you two!" Marlene called from the front steps. "I've hired him for half an hour. I'd like photographs before we eat."

A few photographs were taken of the couple before the carriage, then the parlor fireplace was the backdrop, both with her father and without. Mathais refused to be photographed in his current state of bruising.

At the close of breakfast, Josephine stood. "Thank you, everyone, for celebrating with us this morning. I'm going to change for traveling, but stay as long as you wish—or until my father asks you to leave."

Mr. Wolf laughed. "I took the day off, so don't rush."

Cordelia followed Josephine upstairs.

"Everything was lovely, Jo." She sat on the bed beside Midnight, who was curled on top of Josephine's used nightgown.

"It was, and I'm pleased Cyrus's mother was able to make it." Josephine hung the wedding skirt in the closet and reached for a new blue dress.

"Telephone me when you're ready for visitors," Cordelia said.

"I will, Del. I don't want my move to disrupt our friendship."

After they hugged, Cordelia brought down Josephine's suitcase. Josephine followed carrying Midnight. Rather than stopping to speak to anyone, she went right to the kitchen.

"Will you hold him when we leave, Sarah? I don't want Midnight trying to follow the carriage when we cross Government Street."

"Of course, Jo." She took the cat and they hugged.

"Thank you for being there for me this morning. And the breakfast. Everything was wonderful."

"Are you ready?" Cyrus asked when Josephine entered the parlor.

She nodded and gently hugged her brother. "I expect you to stop by regularly."

"With Sarah as your cook, you'll see me more often than you wish," Mathias said with a subdued smile amid his colorful face.

"Thank you, Papa. I'll be over Sunday afternoon to pick up Midnight." She embraced him and then Marlene. "I appreciate your thoughtfulness in obtaining the photographer."

"You're both too handsome not to capture in portraits."

Cyrus went through his goodbyes and picked up Josephine's suitcase by the door where Cordelia left it. "Thank you all," he said in parting.

Their final carriage ride was to the house, where they would have several hours alone before catching the afternoon ferry.

"What will you do to me when we get home?" she asked Cyrus with a teasing lilt to her voice.

"With such a delicious morsel, I don't know where to begin." He nibbled her neck and then her wrist before their lips fused, not parting until the carriage stopped.

Cyrus had Josephine stay seated until he unlocked the front door and set the luggage inside. Smiling, he tipped the driver, carried her up the porch stairs, and brought his bride over the threshold.

THE END

Author's Note

As usual, I have a list of people who helped me along my journey. Diving back into the world of Mobile's Progressive Era is like going home after fifteen novels and numerous short stories set during this time period, and I'm blessed my family is still supportive of my literary journeys.

I try to represent the people in my character-driven stories with insight, honesty, and candor. Research, interviews, and observation are all part of my process. This time around, Stephanie Thompson did me a great service by doing a sensitivity read as I traveled waters previously unexplored on my literary ramblings. I appreciate your insight and encouragement.

Jennifer Lamont, my beta reader, helped me see where the story needed clarifying and broadening. Plus, she named Cordelia Barnes. Thanks for caring for the characters and being a great sounding board for improvements.

Candice Marley Conner, my long-time critique partner, sticks with me even when my characters take new paths—sometimes multiple ones on the same project. Thank you for being there for my editorial freak outs.

I'm proud to once again have an Amanda Manley original watercolor grace the cover of my book. Amanda's Gothic whimsy is perfect for Josephine and her spiritual wanderings—and Midnight! Thank you for another gorgeous piece.

And last, to keep him humble, the amazing Sean Connell—editor extraordinaire. He is one of the only people who will stand up to my characters when they jump the plot rails. He constantly knows how and when to push me to give my stories their best shot at success. Thanks, Boss.